Gone On Kauai

A Karl Standt Novel

Bruce W. Perry

Web Dispatches Publishing

Cover design by LLPix Designs and
Laura LaRoche

ISBN 9780692740927

**Email the author if you wish:
bruce.perry.author@gmail.com**

This book is dedicated to two great avid readers,
my children Rachel and Scott Perry

More Fiction by Bruce W. Perry:

To The North (New!!) (In 2025, Brad Garner ventures north towards the Yellowstone volcanic epicenter to find a survivor, as well as redemption. Perry offers another darkly rich angle with To the North, a heart-wrenching story of loss and hopelessness following a devastating super volcano eruption. *Self Publishing Review*, 2018)

Atomic Night (New!!) (Chad Kidd, who bombs around the desert on a Kawasaki KLR650 and sips Milagro Silver to blow off steam, decides to take on a cold case involving the murdered daughter of his old police pal. An "outback noir" that takes place mostly in Palm Springs and the desert.)

Accidental Exiles (A young Iraq veteran flees the Middle Eastern wars to Europe–available in paperback and ebook. "A genuine pleasure to read. It is hard not to respect any author who is able to capture the terror and heartbreaking nature of war, while also detailing the delicate heartbreak of missed chances and lost love, and Perry achieves both with a deftly-subtle hand. The tone is consistent, the pacing is perfect, and the plot is striking in a way that fiction often lacks." *Self Publishing Review*, 2017)

Ascent (An adventure story of survival and redemption)

Barbarous Coasts (The first book in the Karl Standt crime thriller series)

Compulsion (The third book in the Karl Standt series. Two detectives pursue a serial killer working through a dating agency. "The book's great strength is its characters." *Crime Fiction Lover*)

Journey By Fire (Armed with a crossbow, Mike Wade roams the dystopian USA deserts in search of his captive daughter Kara. This "tautly told tale turns out to be a vibrant addition to the genre... an effective odyssey through a burned, blighted future America." *Kirkus Reviews*, 2017)

Guilt (A sinister mystique seems to haunt three American businessmen when they hire a guide to take them into the Swiss Alps. "A fast-paced and engaging novella with an intriguingly dramatic twist." *Self Publishing Review*, 2017)

Devastated Lands (Young people fight to survive an eruption of Mt. Rainier. "A thrilling story set in an unforgiving landscape, as well as a personal drama of Shane Cooper, who is torn between his purely selfish need for survival and equally strong need to help others...an entertaining post-apocalyptic adventure pitting man versus nature." *IndieReader review*, 2017)

Lost Young Love (A coming-of-age story about a man's younger affairs with women. "This uniquely themed work will make you blush, laugh, and … remember your own early stumbles and triumphs in the realm of young love." *Self Publishing Review*, Aug. 2017)

CHAPTER 1: MISSING

You probably know the type—blond, bikini-clad, early twenties, they stroll down to the white-sand beach in front of the St. Regis Princeville in Kauai, but never before noon.

For some reason they come in threes: triplet blonds heading straight for the St. Regis booth guy who hands out the voluminous, flawlessly white towels. Then they settle into reserved chaise lounges facing Hanalei Bay.

They peel away the thin, throw-over-the-bikini layer, and spend most of the afternoon soaking up the sun, changing positions in the chaise, and poking at their cell phones to answer the text feed on last night's romantic imbroglios.

The sun can't make them any prettier; it can only touch up and accentuate what they already have.

Down the row at the St. Regis might be the Saudi prince, poking at his own phone, looking distracted, not quite having fun in the sun and somewhat over-dressed for the occasion, for when you have *that* much money, not even the St. Regis and Kauai seems fun anymore.

Amanda Wilcox looked like one of those blonds, but she wasn't a card-carrying member of their club. She may have gone to the St. Regis, but mainly to rent a stand-up paddleboard and take it out for a spin on Hanalei Bay.

She had long, sun-lightened blond hair, a healthy tan, and a female surfer's physique. She wore the sleek one-piece bathing suits of an athlete.

One late afternoon, about four p.m., she took her board out on the water off of Pu'u Poa Beach, heading toward the river and the Bay. A spectacular sunset unfolded over the water in a couple of hours.

The dark-haired kid who fetched her board watched her paddle away, and maybe a few strangers on the beach.

Only the paddleboard came back. A fisherman found it that early evening banging up against the black volcanic rocks of Sealodge Beach, around the point from Hanalei Bay.

Everyone who met Amanda Wilcox liked her. They wanted to *be* like her. They couldn't help it. She exuded an irresistible combination of beauty, eagerness, and humility.

Now everyone was looking for Amanda.

CHAPTER 2: THE FEEDING FRENZY

Karl Standt had heard about her. The missing-Amanda story from Hawaii had hit the tabloids and spread virally through every news conduit, especially the loud and hyperbolic ones.

It fit a formula that the media conglomerates loved–she was bright, photogenic, innocent, young, and missing in the tropics. People couldn't get enough of the news coverage.

A middle-aged tourist had drowned while snorkeling off the Napali Coast on Kauai during the same weekend, and another person had driven their pick-up off the road and into a tree on the West Shore of the island, but those tragedies were completed dominated and superseded by Amanda's.

The victims weren't young, smart, and well enough connected to make the cover of the *Daily News* or to lead off every edition of CNN and Fox. Their deaths didn't convey the same degree of equatorial suspense: a shark attack, a predatory dalliance, a young innocent woman in the tropics giving way to her temptations, bringing on evil deeds, as though the deeds were a pestilence incorporated into the wild undergrowth of the landscape itself.

As a retired NYPD detective and private investigator in Manhattan, Standt read the story in the *Daily News* one morning with more than a casual interest. He sat with his coffee and the paper unfolded in front of him. He was in one of his regular Midtown diners, but the waiters moving quickly between the booths and the surrounding chatter faded from his mind as he fixated on the story.

She'd been alone when she went off on her board that afternoon (only the dark-haired kid, basically a beach rat, as a witness) and the body hadn't been found for at least the first forty-eight hours. Bad news, he thought, on both fronts.

The paucity of evidence about what had happened to her had unleashed wild speculation. The narratives were lurid and silly in inverse proportion to the availability of real information. All of it was probably wrong, he knew from experience. And she was from the New York area–she'd gone to an elite private high school uptown.

She was a classmate and friend of the star actress Turner Espray; then she had gone on to graduate from Vassar College with a degree in biology. She was only twenty-six-years-old at the time she disappeared on Kauai.

The *Daily News* story had interviewed the father Sam Wilcox, a legal deacon and prominent lawyer in Manhattan. Standt knew of him from other newspaper accounts, pictures of him appearing at red-carpet symphonies and star-studded fundraising soirees. He'd worked on the staff of Eliot Spitzer when the latter was governor, and once almost ran for U.S. Senator from New York.

Standt felt sorry for the well-known dad. That was unusual–he commonly could care less about the foibles that unfolded in the lives of celebrities and other members of the entitled set, whose out-of-control behavior seemed to be squandering their own money and everyone else's time.

Yet, daughters were different. Standt didn't have one; he had one son. But he could empathize with Wilcox's ordeal. The man had to deal with his private demons, and perhaps worse, a shallow and insatiable media, frothing at the mouth over another family's misfortune. All they cared about was goosing their ratings and getting their viewers begging for more.

Cable news led off their broadcasts with splashy, intrusive headlines like "Where's Amanda?" To them, she was an attractive, All-American type poster girl who is somehow permitted to be referred to by only her first name. There was something obscene about the overfamiliarity, as though the news producers were suddenly cozy with her.

Missing young children were worse of these cases. He couldn't imagine what Wilcox was going through.

# # #

The media was trying to shoehorn Amanda Wilcox's disappearance into the same formula as the case of the beautiful, missing young high school graduate from the south named Ashley Hedgeland.

Hedgeland had gone missing in the Caribbean resort island of Aruba in 2007. It was a particularly abhorrent and sleazy case that was never solved, a cold case. It gave off a stink of corruption and incompetence among the Dutch authorities who ran Aruba. The principal suspect in the Hedgeland case was a spoiled, sociopathic young Dutchman named Joran.

They had really screwed that case up. There was evidence of a cover-up among Aruban justice authorities because this Joran character was well-connected. He was later prosecuted for killing another young woman in Peru, and he was now rotting in a South American jail. The fates had caught up with the young psychopath, but not soon enough to help poor Ashley Hedgeland, who'd found herself at the wrong party with the wrong man at the wrong time.

Ashley had nothing to do with Amanda, except that both cases involved pretty young white women who'd gone missing in the tropics under mysterious circumstances. They fit a formula that the media Kahunas loved.

Sam Wilcox was in Kauai, Hawaii trying to find out what happened to his daughter, and Standt could imagine what dealing with that was like, as a parent with no police-work experience. Wilcox was caught in a complex morass involving the local authorities (often incompetent with complicated, far-from open-and-shut cases), and an unfamiliar local culture to boot.

It was just about then, when Standt was pondering this case on the *Daily News* pages, that he got an email on his cell phone from a *New York Post* reporter he knew named Don Latham.

Standt was well-known around New York as a crack no-nonsense investigator who got things done. He wrapped up cases, and was particularly adept at prying open cold ones. Latham had written a story about the missing Wilcox and interviewed her father, who out of the blue asked the reporter whether he knew of a really good Manhattan investigator.

Wilcox wanted to hire a crack P.I. to help him find his daughter on Kauai. Latham had immediately suggested Standt. Wilcox was at his wit's end, and he was smart enough to seek outside help.

CHAPTER 3: LATHAM

Standt reached Latham in the busy *New York Post* newsroom. He heard muffled keyboard typing and remarks in the background, then Latham's hungover voice, which sounded like he was talking through a pillow.

"How goes the battle Karl?"

"Don, is that really you? You don't sound like you got your four hours of beauty sleep last night."

"Hey, I got at least five…besides, I had more important things to do than sleep."

"Like what?"

"Like…live my life as if there's no tomorrow. As Jon Bon Jovi and the poet Robert Lowell would advocate."

"I think they expressed that belief in very different ways…"

"But you get the point." Latham sounded like he typically looked; thinning and unkempt hair, unshaven, bagged eyes, never without some kind of sports cap pulled tightly over his forehead. Standt suddenly thought of Latham as a kind of orphan, with no one around to take care of him. He knew he wasn't married and both of his parents had died; Standt's Mom was still alive, in Vermont. Latham meant well and had a good heart.

"Two things," Standt asked, before he got down to brass tacks. "Where was the watering hole, and how were their tequila cocktails, on a Rotten Tomatoes scale?"

"The Pink Elephant Club, and about a fifty-five. So you got my message? About Wilcox?"

"I did. And thanks for making the connection."

"No worries. He's hot to hire a detective. And believe me, he'll pay."

"He's missing his daughter. That seems to be the main point."

"Yeah but, he can afford to pay good wages, if you know what I mean. Everyone has to make a living."

Standt would almost have taken the case *pro bono*, he'd gotten so worked up reading about it. The waiter came by and nestled a plate of scrambled eggs and bacon next to the *Daily News*, and Standt signaled thanks to him.

"I know about the case," he said. "It's a sad one; actually, fucked up as in mismanaged. In fact, I'm reading about it right now in your competitor's paper."

As a reporter, Latham had a sixth sense for exposing the seedier stories. They came naturally to him, and he was comfortable wading into those murky, polluted waters, so to speak. In fact, if you took away his license to party, smoke, and frequent Lower East Side sex clubs, then his journalistic mojo was in danger of being defanged.

But this was a new kind of story that Latham had latched on to, only because of Wilcox's reputation in Manhattan, and his daughter's popularity. There was even a rumor that the movie star Turner Espray had wanted to get directly involved, to help find her old school-mate and friend.

Espray had called into a CNN special report to talk about how horrible and predatory the social atmosphere could be for young women in high places.

Of course, all these connections–Amanda, Turner, Wilcox, the tony tropical ambiance, and the gruesome allure of a possible shark attack (the prevailing theory, so far)–made great fodder for the New York tabloids.

"Is he still in Hawaii? Wilcox?"

"Yeah. You're going to hear from him any moment now. I gave him your email."

"Okay. Much appreciated. So this means he'll want me to come to Hawaii?"

"Yup, Kauai. Tough assignment, huh? Mai tais, hula dancers, sunsets, Bali Hai…"

"Sounds like you want to go."

"I'd love to, buddy. What a spot for a boots-on-the ground story!"

Standt still only had tabloid knowledge of the Amanda Wilcox case. He knew even less about Kauai. He had never been to Hawaii, or even San Diego or San Francisco. He would have to do some research beforehand. The young lanky hacker, Church, could help him with that.

Maybe Wilcox would agree to bankroll Church's presence in Kauai. Standt's imagination had already leapt forward, before he'd even hung up on the reporter. Yet, Standt couldn't imagine the emaciated, six-foot-nine Church fitting in with surfers, Polynesian dancers, and copper-colored tans.

He knew that the Amanda case was frozen in place, and the clock was ticking.

It was usually very bad news when missing-person cases weren't solved within the first twenty-four hours. The younger the person was, the worse the news would often get.

But Amanda was twenty-six years old, so this case had different angles and permutations compared with one involving a missing child.

Latham would be one of the people to talk to about the finer points of her disappearance. He'd written a couple of follow-ups about it.

"Anything new with the case? What's going on?"

"That's what I was going to ask you." Latham sounded older than he was (about thirty-nine). With his receding gray hair, tough-guy voice, and mirthful manner, Latham was a throw-back to the old-time reporters who'd grind out a crime-beat story then toss down the whiskeys afterward.

Although by now, he'd moved on to fancy cognac and tequila. He was aware of his existence as a dying breed; as the print newspaper business was close to going extinct.

"How come the *Post* hasn't sent you there?"

"Kauai?"

"Yeah."

"Are you kidding me? The accounting department gives me crap about the expense reports I send them for cabs and meals in Manhattan. The cheap bastards. They think you can write any story from a Midtown desk. You gotta put boots on the ground where a story's breaking, if you know what I mean. You gotta get into the weeds. The *Post* might send me to Hawaii if the Pope got kidnapped there.

"But yeah, the Amanda case has apparently run aground. For us and the investigators."

"In what way?"

"No body still. No leads. Or suspects the local police are talking about. Not that they know what the fuck they're doing."

"The information seems hearsay," Standt said. "It really reminds me of the Hedgeland case. Nothing's solid. It's all wishy-washy, murky, anecdotal."

The fact that the sophisticated lawyer father was getting desperate told Standt something.

"Yeah. This story's kind of fizzling out," Latham said. He held the phone away and coughed spasmodically. "Beyond the aftermath-of-the-death type angles. People with fond memories, and the like. They think she drowned, or got chewed up by a shark. Or both."

Standt sensed the shudder of anxiety in his bones. It was a mixture of sadness, regret, and morbid fear. He'd been on too many cases that involved innocent young female victims of violent crimes.

In addition, he'd never really liked the ocean, and the unseen creatures beneath it, especially sharks. He still remembered the time he ran into that huge barracuda in Bermuda.

"They haven't found the body though? Any body? Any physical evidence?"

"No way. It's all circumstantial. It seems like a shark attack, or accidental drowning. Sam Wilcox is a total disbeliever."

"Why? Is it denial? He wants to believe his daughter is still alive?"

"There's probably a little of that psychology. And other problems. No body, no evidence; too obvious a conclusion. A shark attack is assumed for anyone who doesn't come back from the tropical ocean. She was on one of those surfboards people stand on."

"Paddleboards," Standt said. He'd actually tried one on the Hudson. He wanted to do it again.

"When did you talk to Sam Wilcox?"

"Last night."

"What did he say exactly?"

"That the case is totally fucked up. The investigation.

He didn't use those words, but he's a smart guy. He knows fuck-up when he sees it. And it's his daughter. He needs help."

Standt breathed easy, imagining himself on Kauai. He'd pursued felons in Switzerland and Dubai before, two other exotic realms for a Vermont and New York guy.

"Well, thanks for giving him my name. I owe you one. Dinner. Victuals in Manhattan, something other than copious amounts of booze."

Standt didn't want to get caught up in another big party with Latham. That would definitely wipe out the next day. As a former problem drinker, he never was not an alcoholic. At least that was the therapeutic paradigm. He found that approach kind of defeatist; a true bummer. At any rate, he had to watch the booze.

"The other thing with Amanda…" Latham said. "There's probably a guy, a dude involved. I'd pursue that thread." Standt thought of Hedgeland and the Aruba case, the ultimate fiasco. Beautiful young women in the tropics, opening up to ambitious young playboys and sybarites. That added up to a perilous cocktail.

"She had everything–looks, smarts, sensitivity. A real tragedy. A heartbreaker." Latham's voice trailed off, with about as much wistfulness as he could muster.

The gears were churning inside Standt. He was hoping the case wasn't just a body hunt.

CHAPTER 4: THE BOYFRIEND

Standt logged on to Gmail and found the message from Wilcox. It was succinct, to the point. Although he innately mistrusted the motivations of someone who held that much power and influence, Standt liked that Wilcox's note didn't pull any punches:

Dear Detective Karl Standt,

I am Amanda Wilcox's father. We are trying to find her on Kauai, Hawaii, since she disappeared on June 15. I believe the investigation is deeply flawed and has been seriously led astray. Don Latham tells me you're a crack investigator, one of Manhattan's best. I am willing to pay your fee, travel expenses, and put you up in our time-share in Princeville (the vicinity of Kauai where she was last seen). Please help me find out what happened to my daughter. I will admit I am at my wit's end. If interested, I will send you a check as a downpayment and all the information you need for centering an investigation on Kauai. Respond using this email.

Very truly yours, Sam Wilcox, Esquire.

Standt fired back a message:

Dear Sam Wilcox,

I am deeply sorry that your daughter Amanda has been missing. I'd be honored to take on your case. I can start as soon as Monday. Please send along the information about Kauai.

Sincerely, Karl Standt.

He concluded by leaving his address, a small Manhattan loft at 20th Street and Eighth Avenue.

# # #

It was a Friday night in the third week of June when Standt exchanged these messages. Things came together fast. He was scheduled to fly out of JFK to Lihue Airport in Kauai on Monday.

However, he received a second message related to Amanda Wilcox not soon after the email exchange with her father. This time it came from her boyfriend, a man about her age named Dash Crenshaw. He lived in Manhattan. He told Standt in the message that he worked in finance for a big firm and was "very close" to the missing woman.

Crenshaw was a little pushy. He wanted to talk to Standt about Amanda first. The detective's name was circulating among the unseen network of Wilcox connections, now that Standt was the big dog in the search. As a veteran of the Midtown Detective Bureau, now retired, Standt knew the big-city types all too well. As in, *my agenda occupies the center of the universe right now.*

Maybe Standt could learn something from this Crenshaw.

Everyone seemed desperate about the integrity of the case, beginning with Latham. It was common knowledge that the search for Amanda had been completely botched.

# # #

Standt walked to Midtown from his loft in Chelsea on a breezy, sunny day in the city. The air smelled cleansed and the sun flared brightly from behind the buildings. He often looked for excuses to walk to meetings, especially on days like this, and didn't always opt for the Yellow Cabs, subways, or black-and-white cruisers to get around.

He'd told the young man to meet him at a city diner called The Madison Restaurant on East 53rd Street at First Avenue.

He spotted Crenshaw waiting for him on the wide, busy sidewalk in front of the restaurant. Crenshaw was a tall, good-looking kid with neatly trimmed black hair who reminded Standt of the young Mel Gibson in the 1980s movie, *Year Of Living Dangerously*.

Crenshaw met Standt with a smile and shook his hand firmly before they went into the diner.

He had the unshakeable optimism of a young man, veering towards wishful naivete, Standt thought. First impressions, but he could start to get to know Amanda by the vibes he picked up from Crenshaw. Many cases took surreal turns. A woman is lost in the North Pacific, but hardly anyone who knows her sees it as a cut-and-dried drowning case.

They took a booth next to a window. Standt loved diners and window seats, from where he could peaceably watch the world stream by. He spent a serious amount of time in the Plaza Diner at Second Avenue and 56th, as well as the Madison. The Spanish waiters all knew who he was.

"I wanted to talk to you about Amanda before you

left for Hawaii," Crenshaw said, wide-eyed and earnest. "Who have you talked to already?"

Sometimes missing-person cases became politicized among the family members. Standt wondered what Crenshaw's true agenda was, and he didn't feel like becoming the family referee.

"I've emailed with her father," Standt said. "Why do you want to know?"

"That's all?"

"That's all."

"I want to know because most of the stories about her are dead wrong. Total bullshit!"

"I get where you're coming from, from what little I know."

"That's good. That's good."

His square jaw was set and his green eyes glared. The usual sleazy romance stories supposedly involving Amanda were bandied about in the tabloids, as though she was a Lohan or Kardashian.

"How long have you known her?"

"About six months."

"Where did you meet?"

"At a mixer. The Hudson Union Society. Downtown."

"So six months…" This fella looked like marrying bait. Works for a big bank, makes big bucks, handsome, smart.

He doesn't seem sad enough, though. He seems more interested in having his opinions made known.

"How serious were you two?"

"We were pretty serious. We both travel a lot. We weren't always together, but we weren't seeing other people, if that's what you mean. At least I'm sure *I* wasn't."

The press stories included rumors about a man or

men Amanda might have been seeing on Kauai. She was active on the social circuit; Kauai apparently had an overheated one.

"What makes you think Amanda wasn't loyal to you?"

"I'm 99 percent sure she wasn't. Cheating. She wasn't the type to play around, like some of these sleazy tabloids have implied."

Now some passion surfaces. Love, or at least devotion and loyalty.

He sipped a cup of tea with lemon; he had a salmon salad on the way. Crenshaw ordered coffee and a brownie sundae. He wondered how Crenshaw hung on to his Mel Gibson looks with that kind of diet. *Ah, youth.*

"Where were you on the day she disappeared?"

No one had brought Crenshaw up as a suspect. In cases of missing or murdered women, the husband or the boyfriend ends up guilty of the crime about nine times out of ten.

They'd probably written him off as soon as it was known he wasn't around Hawaii during Amanda's fateful paddleboard ride.

"I was in New York working. When they found out she was missing, I went to Kauai. Three days. A couple of local cops, real yokels, say she got killed by a shark. They never found her body," he said contemptuously.

"And what's wrong with *that* conclusion?"

"The local cops picked the easiest conclusion to draw. They're just lazy and incompetent. They deal with too many drowning cases in Kauai. They just lumped Amanda in with the others." He talked faster and faster as his ire rose.

"…No one's committed to the case. I was shocked. I went into the station, and they wouldn't show me the paddleboard. The one with the supposed shark bites. They said it was protected evidence. I'm glad Sam brought you in."

So he's on first-name basis with the rich dad. Okay. Crenshaw was a bright guy who essentially agreed with Latham and Sam Wilcox; the case of Amanda's disappearance was in total fucked-up mode.

"...She was an excellent swimmer, and respected the ocean. I'm not saying she couldn't have been killed by a shark, but something about that conclusion doesn't sit right. It fails the sniff test, if you know what I mean."

"Sure."

"When you think Amanda, you don't think drowning, and taking unnecessary risks."

"What do *you* think happened to her?"

Crenshaw's sundae arrived, and he put his head down and launched into devouring it like a man who hadn't eaten in days. He must swim about 20,000 yards a day, Standt thought, to keep a flat belly like that. Or maybe it's that hyperactivity I detect.

"I think it's possible..." He was having trouble getting the next thought out, and Standt thought it was because Crenshaw was conscious of its possible flakiness.

"...that she was killed for what she had found out."

"What was Amanda *doing* in Kauai?"

Now things were getting interesting.

CHAPTER 5: GMO IN THE BLOODSTREAM

"She was an activist monitoring the GMO industry."

"GMO?"

"Genetically Modified Organism. Changing the DNA of seeds and crops to make new food. It's big on the island; there are corporate labs on Kauai that are heavily into GMO research. Monsanto, others. It's very controversial and unpopular among the locals, not to mention a lot of other people. It's viewed as a form of contamination, similar to rampant pesticide use. Messing with Mother Nature.

"Amanda worked…works…for a non-profit organization called PFW. Pure Food World. They're anti-GMO campaigners."

Standt immediately thought it was kind of strange that a big-finance guy would be into a do-gooder lady, a non-profiter, and vice versa. If she was a passionate anti-corporate type, what did she see in Crenshaw, beyond the dreamy eyes, square jaw, and leading-man hair?

"How long had she been in Kauai?"

"Two months. At least."

"Did she ever talk to you about it?"

"A little bit. Not in detail. She told me she was finding out about a lot of things. Corruption within the industry."

"Huh."

Standt personally viewed the U.S. and its corporations as awash in fraud and corruption. Maybe Crenshaw, and Amanda, *were* on to something.

"What kind of corruption?"

"Well, you know. Testing organisms with no oversight. Using the island as a guinea pig. Bribes and graft…"

"What kind of bribes?"

"Pay-offs and kick-backs. To local regulators. USDA."

"Wow. Did she tell anyone else about this?"

"No. I think she was planning to though."

"Does her father know about it?"

"I don't think so. He wasn't necessarily into what she was doing. In terms of taking a hands-on interest."

"Why not?"

"He thought it was flaky, I think. Knee-jerk anti-corporate stuff."

Crenshaw said that in a way that made it more his opinion than Sam Wilcox's. Maybe he'd had a few spats about that issue with his girlfriend.

"Do you have a picture of Amanda on you?"

"Yeah, as a matter of fact…"

"I've only seen the newspaper stuff."

"That's okay." Crenshaw dug into his wallet and

handed Standt a photo of both of them. They were standing on a ferry together, a super sharp couple in sunglasses.

Their plates and cups were now empty. Standt chewed down his salad while Crenshaw was talking. He was wondering what Dash was going to do with all these incriminating innuendos.

"Do you have any of the documentation on what Amanda was digging up?"

"No. That's the other thing. I haven't been able to get a hold of her personal belongings. Her laptop."

"Her father will be able to take care of that," Standt said.

"Mr. Standt…"

"Call me Karl. Or, detective, if you want."

"Okay, Karl."

Crenshaw looked earnest, his jaw set. "I wish you would take all this into account in your investigation. I think it will lead to something, the GMO connection. I think something's happened to her…Someone got to her."

"I'm going to Kauai on Monday. What did you say the name of her organization was, the NGO?"

"Pure Food World. They have a web page."

They both stood up to leave. Crenshaw quickly took care of the check. Then they sidled their way through the chatty crowd in the diner and out on to First Avenue, where the hot air of summer hit them like an anvil. The city was getting hotter, Standt thought, by the hour.

A man with a dolly unloaded boxes of produce from a truck, and the street was noisy and clogged with activity. Parts of the sidewalk were hosed-down clean; others were sticky with rotten and spoiled vegetables from all the vendors delivering their wares.

"Detective…" Crenshaw said, shooting a suspicious glance both ways on the humid avenue. He'd loosened his tie, the shirt collar open. His eyes were bright and misty.

"Find Amanda. Please. Find out what happened to her. I miss her. We all do. She didn't deserve this…whatever happened to her. I think you'll find my information useful. Will you contact me if you find out anything? Will you contact me anyways, next week? Here's my card, for cell phone and email."

"Sure thing. Likewise, keep me informed," Standt said. "If anything else comes up."

Then Crenshaw turned and walked briskly away. He was a big meeting guy, Standt thought, and the detective was just another contact for him. But Dash's eyes had showed some passion just then, not quite as much as Standt would have wanted from a man whose lover may have been devoured by an apex predator. Or otherwise died violently.

The sun glared off a windowed tower that loomed over First Avenue. Standt still had to buy his plane tickets. The air was humid and choked with diesel exhaust from an idling delivery truck.

New York City was heating up for a Friday night, but Standt was certain the atmosphere would be hotter in Kauai. He headed west on 53rd to hoof it back down Fifth Avenue to his loft. He thought of white sands and gorgeous sunsets amidst the clanging car horns and frenetic crowds.

CHAPTER 6: AN EGG-WHITE YACHT

A large, egg-shell white yacht sat in the ocean off the northeast coast of Kauai and Hanalei Bay. A steady, pulsating stream of catchy pop music carried over the water from the twinkling cluster of lights off-shore. The yacht bristled with radar dishes and antennae, more laden with hi-tech equipment than any Coast Guard vessel.

People milled about the decks of the well-appointed vessel, the tan women in pearls and flattering, tropical summer dresses, the men looking like snotty country-club sailors, except for the waiters, who were in tails.

The people danced and gyrated next to the rails, below which the luminescent water lapped placidly against the hull.

The alcohol and Champagne flowed. The waiters passed around hors d'oeuvres, including ono sushi from the surrounding waters, Russian caviar, and duck parfait. Pieces of hors d'oeuvres littered the deck, discarded in places by patrons who didn't like the taste of the first nibble, and even tumbling from the flapping lower lips of others.

The DJ put on more techno music, and before he turned up the volume, peals of laughter and shouted conversation could be heard over the blue-green water. Since the cruise ships, which looked like floating cities that were about to tip over into the drink, had passed on, the yacht was by far the largest vessel anchored off Kauai. It was once featured in *Forbes* magazine.

Costing more than half a billion, the vessel included three gourmet restaurants, a fully equipped gym and spa, and a helipad. All these lavish amenities were paid for entirely by Monsanto Corporation, whose accountants had made sure that the 2012 United States tax bill for the corporation was *zero.*

This was a fact that Ted Rand liked to gleefully repeat to his friends. He was a Monsanto Executive VP who was wont to spend a lot of his time on the yacht, ferrying between the Hawaiian islands.

He was the head of Monsanto's GMO division. Much experimentation was going on in Hawaii concerning new, lucrative seed DNA.

"There's gold in them thar seeds," was another quote that Rand liked to repeat, along with the one about Monsanto's goose-egg 2012 tax bill.

# # #

Rand stood by the railing and watched the equatorial sun slip into the ocean like a vast bonfire off the Napali Coast. He wore neatly creased white linen shorts, sandals, and a button-down blue-striped shirt.

Sheer cliffs and vaporous, dark-green jungle rose like a rug from the aquamarine sea, which glistened in the sunlight cresting at the horizon.

"Where else do you get a view like that?" Ted posed the question to his wife, Betsy Rand. "God's country. God's own coast." *Everything that money can buy*, he mused to himself. Including the over-the-top yacht and frequent lavish views like this one.

Rand sipped on Champagne. He'd already been through about a bottle of it. A Chateau Margaux was in the on-deck circle, ready to accompany the Maki filet.

"Absolutely *beautiful*," Betsy crooned. "Do they allow any building over there? It's so remote and untouched."

"No," Ted barked, as if rebuking a child. "It's protected coastline. Conservation land; all of it." Not even the man with the untrammeled free-market views and free reign over a garish yacht wanted the Napali Coast developed.

"You want to be able to sail past there and not look at some Chinese factory owner's eye-sore."

"I *love* sailing," Betsy said wistfully. She leaned into the railing, the waters lapping calmly below. "When are we going sailing again? I can't wait."

This is sailing enough for me, Rand thought to himself. He preferred it; he was too lazy and his skills too crude for real sailing. "Maybe soon." He was also buzzed, which made his comments lean towards the patronizing.

He gave his wife's figure a wolfish scan. They'd had a few sex parties on-board, which she'd be none too pleased to hear about, if she knew about them in the first place. Her own figure had been "augmented" at thirty-five.

The dress dipped beneath the tan line above her breasts. He let his eyes linger on her cleavage for the length of time it took Betsy to notice him.

The music played, tinnily over the water. Then he began swiveling his hips, awkwardly holding the fluted glass with an out-stretched right hand. The drink sloshed back and forth like a stormy sea, then some of it splashed onto the deck. Betsy took the clumsy motion to be some kind of silly, and not very arousing, mating ritual.

The rest of the people on the deck were acting vapid in more or less direct proportion to their place on the corporate hierarchy. Betsy had a graduate degree herself in organic chemistry from the University of Pennsylvania. She was recruited out of college by Monsanto, where Rand met her as a young up-and-comer himself.

Appearances could be deceiving; she wasn't just a high-suburban fashionista. She was bright, ambitious, and power-hungry, and always had been.

All the pieces fit together into an impressive package for Betsy, and recognizing the same features in himself, this was the element Rand admired the most about his wife.

The beauty of the sea made her think of the missing girl, Amanda Wilcox.

She leaned her elbows on the railing; the yacht dipped and rocked slightly in the swell.

"God, I hope they find her," she murmured, almost to herself. "The poor thing. Isn't it awful? I couldn't imagine…Do you think there's still a possibility that she could be found alive?"

"You mean Wilcox?"

"*Amanda…*"

Rand didn't want to call her Amanda, because the implicit familiarity and femininity took his focus off the eight-ball. It would make him forget about what she was trying to do to Monsanto.

"Not really. It's probably too late now."

"Why? Have they called off the search?"

"The cops are still looking for her. I heard. The Coast Guard stopped several days ago."

For Ted, it was like having someone who dislikes you intensely suddenly drop off the face of the earth.

A. Wilcox–the way he referred to her–had created big-time hassles for his employer. She was turning the GMO issue in Hawaii into a national crusade, and if it got to that point it couldn't be controlled anymore. Control was everything. Billions of dollars were at stake.

Ted found her silence, now that she was missing, downright restful. It was a convenience, as it were. The protests had been grating on him. He'd lost mucho sleep.

Betsy gazed over the railing at the gently lapping waters, as though she was still looking for Amanda. She turned back to Ted for emphasis.

"I hope she's just holed up somewhere with a crewman on a sailboat. She shows up one day; embarrassed, apologetic, and happy."

Betsy found the whole idea of such an escape exhilarating. Monsanto could be a cloying place, incestuous and backbiting, especially if your husband ran everything.

Betsy knew that Amanda hated the company she worked for, and despised what Betsy did for them. Which was to help invent new genes for the basis of food organisms, and plant them–*foist them* would probably be Amanda's term, or worse–on to Hawaii. Frankenseed. Poisons, in the view of the non-profit Pure Food World.

"Here's what I'm going to do, if, when, she's found," Betsy announced, as if it was a revelation. "We're going to take her sailing. She and her boyfriend, if she has one. I'd be surprised if she didn't. What a catch. We're going to take her sailing, and we're going to have an honest discussion about the benefits of GMO science. Absolutely. Sailing has a way of clearing your head. That's how problems are solved."

Rand looked at her skeptically. "She probably hates our guts. Anyways…" he said distantly. "The prospects for her survival are virtually nil. Look, when you disappear off Kauai, and you're not heard from for days, a week…"

He held out his Champagne glass, without looking, and a waiter drifted over and filled it.

Then Rand drank it down with a curt backward tilt of his head. He swallowed hard. "You're probably history. *Done.* You can stick a fork in 'er."

Betsy bristled. "That's disgusting. What a way to put it."

All Ted desired at that moment was to take Betsy back to their stateroom, remove her clothes, and blow off the social twattle with the rest of the Monsanto crowd. He saw them all the time anyways. He wanted to blow off the guests too, including a few DNA scientists, who acted agog at the luxuries of that evening's floating party.

Rand turned away and looked across the deck of the yacht at a group of awkward people with frozen expectant smiles.

"I wish people weren't so anti-science. It's ignorance; that's what it is. Unfounded fears of science; fear of the new and undiscovered. When *is* Monsanto going to learn PR, anyways? Everyone is afraid of GMO. We're the bad guys, the evil GMO Frankensteins.

"Then again, we *do* pay zero taxes." Rand laughed, almost proudly. "Pretty hard to spin that one."

"Right, yeah," Betsy said ruefully. "That's off the point I'm making."

She went on: "It's terrible. I feel sorry for her father. She seemed to be well-meaning. Articulate and bright. She just had strong opinions, and got off on the wrong track. I've known other women like her; she seemed like a young version of them. That's why I wanted to reason with her."

Then they sensed a commotion a ways across the deck. A group of five company men were dancing to the K-Pop hit, *Gangnam Style.* Corporate drones, drunk as lords. Three of them were shirtless and had white, sagging, beer bellies, with splotchy regions of pink sunburn.

A wave of guarded, sporadic laughter flowed over the deck.

Rand chuckled, but held back how hard he really wanted to laugh. He sensed his wife's disapproval. The men were very ugly dancers.

He'd have to get Bruno Reilly to clear the deck. The riffraff were taking over.

"Let's go," he snapped to Betsy, and took her by the elbow with the best grip of a gentleman he could muster. "A private luxury stateroom awaits," he said proudly. "And you can't beat the view of Napali. Not too many rooms have it."

It was more than just a gut feeling he had. A. Wilcox was gone; *Vamonos*.

He swilled the remaining Champagne in his glass as they walked. Things were beginning to look up.

Betsy was quiet. Maybe she wasn't thinking about A. Wilcox anymore.

Big Business has always been a hardball, cutthroat affair. That's just the way it is; the name of the game. Losers and winners; so goes a universal law. Amanda was looking like a loser. She'd made big waves. Sometimes when you do that, like the giants that roll into Hanalei Bay come wintertime, they end up taking *you* down, big time.

CHAPTER 7: NINTENDO HEAVEN

Karl Standt had flown through Phoenix on the way to Lihue Airport in Kauai. The Arizona landscape was awash in relentless sun and dun-colored and its urban development rapidly gave way to vast areas of sandy barrens. It had looked like the desolate moon of a distant star. He stared at the desert out the window, then they landed.

They were instructed to close the window shading and keep the nozzle above their heads open to a stream of cool air, or the aircraft would overheat on the tarmac. It was already 109 Fahrenheit in the early morning. Then he disembarked and wandered the polished hallways of the airport, which resembled a suburban mall, heading for his Kauai connection.

He was renting a car in Lihue Airport and meeting Sam Wilcox in Princeville later that day. He'd left the hacker Church at home. He'd summon the gawky lad later if needed, for his techie, Jack-of-all-trades skills.

For now, the hacker had to clean up his act. He wasn't in particularly good shape when Standt had tracked him down two nights before in Manhattan to brief him on the new case.

He found him with his girlfriend iz at the Midtown Nintendo Center playing video games high as a kite. Standt thought it was Ecstasy, and he was furious. iz (yes, lower-case i) was a fashionable and striking goth-style lady who was the first female ever to really take an interest in Church.

Standt thought a girlfriend would be good for Church, but not if iz pushed him into new realms of addiction. Church was a highly talented NYPD I.T. asset. The hacker had already gone through rehab once with Standt.

At any rate, the detective told Church that his lucrative gig with the NYPD was over if he caught him high again.

# # #

Standt was also seeing someone; a reporter for the news magazine *Slate* who was half his age. It seemed things were looking up for the both he and Church, in the romance department. He was excited to be with Katie, a smart and stunning brunette with much vim and vigor.

Her full name was Katie Putnam. She'd written a story about Standt's skills and bravado tracking down the massive financial felon Max Schmidreiny in Dubai. He'd been shocked when (1) Katie wasn't seeing anyone seriously at the moment, because she was such a hot ticket, and (2) she agreed to go out with him, a retired over-fifty detective still wrestling with booze issues and the accumulated traumas of a violent career.

Katie seemed to understand Standt. Sometimes they would just spend a Sunday reading books and the paper, followed by a nap. Lazy, uncluttered days. He felt almost boring.

But Katie seemed to value his age and superior wisdom–he had about twenty years on her–rather than hold his middle-aged status against him. She'd had a series of either shallow or hurtful, failed affairs; young men in Manhattan kept her on her toes and on edge, whereas with Standt, she could relax, go out to dinner, talk about books and movies, and not worry about living up to some young buck's untested expectations.

Standt was just thrilled to be with her. He more or less expected it to end at any moment. This was very true in the beginning. He had to pinch himself every time he realized that she wanted to spend more time with him.

He eventually invited her to Kauai for a "win win" trip: she could write an edgy story about the Amanda Wilcox disappearance for *Slate*, while exploring the beautiful island. She said she could probably come out later, and was trying to convince her editors to write off the trip, based on the proposed feature article on Amanda.

iz was a different kettle of fish altogether. He found her standing next to Church at the Nintendo Center that night. She was somewhat tall herself with long skinny legs tucked tightly into black jeans, jarringly long silver crucifixes dangling from each ear, and streaky peroxide hair. She had fine, heavily made up facial features–lipstick so red it was almost black–very Lower East Side chic.

If she was anything, she was compelling. At least Church had a life partner for the time being, but Standt was going to have to keep an eye on him.

CHAPTER 8: PRINCEVILLE BLUFF

Sam Wilcox's condo was located on a bluff overlooking the North Pacific.

Standt rented a car at Lihue Airport, and then drove along the island's east coast to the north shore of Kauai.

Off to his left shoulder as he drove, in the center of the island, the sun shone in floating yellow regions on the lush, dark-green lower flanks of a 5,000-foot mountain that ascended into seemingly permanent dark gray clouds. The mountain seemed primeval; the clouds like giant black anvils.

The tallest mountain sat in the center of Kauai and received a deluge of rain, but the fringes of the island and its white-sand beaches had plenty of sunshine.

Standt turned off the main road into the entrance to the tony Princeville development. He passed a large marble statue and fountain, then went down a road that was bordered by a nice park on one side and a golf course and residences on the other.

Then he took a right on Kamehameha Road. Just before the sign for the Sealodge units, he took another right and parked his rental in the small lot.

He was a little cooked by traveling, but he was looking forward to meeting Wilcox.

He walked across the lot, where the sun baked the newly tarred surface, and around to the back of the condo. He found Sam sitting on a fold-out chair on the bluff silently looking out over the ocean.

A cooling breeze wafted up from the sea. There were small bushes with red fragrant flowers growing on the edge of the grass. Tall healthy palm trees swayed above, loaded with coconuts that looked just about ready to drop.

The flat ocean beneath the bluff shimmered in the noon-day sun. Mushroom shaped white and gray storm clouds crept across the distant horizon, hung with curtains of rain.

Wilcox stood up slowly when Standt, immediately feeling over-dressed for the Hawaiian sun, padded across the grass.

Wilcox gave off an air of near resignation. His mouth was set and he moved his old, lean limbs wearily when he came over to shake Standt's hand. The detective knew that he was probably the lawyer's last resort.

"You must be the detective."

"Karl Standt."

"Sam Wilcox."

"You have a beautiful spot here." In fact, Standt may never have seen a better view since his adventures in the Alps.

Wilcox looked out toward the ocean impassively; its visual beauty had all but vanished for him. He wouldn't recover it until he found out what happened to his daughter.

At any rate, he had no comment about the condo's

view, startling and memorable for any unassuming visitor. Wilcox simply nodded his head as though the deluxe view was meaningless (which it was at the moment for him), then said: "Please, take a chair." An empty fold-out chair sat next to his own.

"Can I get you a drink?"

"Well…" Standt made a quick calculation about the time of day. It was just past noon. He used to be a drunk.

"Are you?"

A smile crept up the old lawyer's bony cheek, replacing the sad reserve. Standt could sense some of the barrister's shrewdness, his years at the bar. But the intelligence was leavened by a courtliness and charm; he was an old-school city lawyer with powerful clients.

None of the legal fame or unerring instincts, however, had prevented his beautiful daughter from disappearing.

"Yes, I am. Wine. Red or white?"

"White." Standt would nurse it.

"I'll have white too. When I'm in the city, it's red."

"I'm that way too."

Wilcox moved to the sliding glass door and went inside the condo to fetch the drinks. He had white hair that was neatly trimmed and his face and arms were tan. He wore a short-sleeved shirt and light-checkered shorts and sandals.

Standt had the impression that when he'd first shown up, he had interrupted the old man's reverie, a long drawn-out remembrance that Wilcox was having while staring at the ocean.

The horizon stretched uninterrupted by another land mass maybe all the way to the Aleutians, and the sea, topped with thousands of tiny white waves that Standt had seen from the plane, frothed over a nearby reef.

Standt wondered when the palms were going to drop their coconuts.

"The view *is* nice, isn't it?" It was Wilcox coming outside with the two drinks. He made the comment as though he had to be reminded of how far you could see from the top of the bluff.

Standt found his manner warm, even though the detective was a stranger. Yet, in Wilcox's eyes, Standt was also the man who might find Amanda, or at least help define the final chapter of her legacy. Maybe this was why Wilcox already seemed like an old friend.

He had that way about him.

He handed Standt his white wine. Standt leapt up and closed the sliding door behind Sam.

"Thank you. Please, take a seat."

Wilcox sat down and took a sip of his wine before he spoke.

"I know you've just stepped off the plane, and you must be a little sapped."

"I'm not bad."

"Where did you fly through?"

"Phoenix."

"Good," he said approvingly.

"But we'll have to start right away with the business at hand. Amanda's disappearance."

"Absolutely."

"You'll stay here of course."

"Where are you staying?"

"I'm at the St. Regis, right now. It's down the road."

"Oh."

"That's where Amanda was last seen you know, when she left on a paddleboard."

"Who saw her?"

"The kid who rents the equipment down there. He was the last one to see her alive…" He coughed uncontrollably, then composed himself quickly.

Wilcox recrossed his legs and looked down at his feet, moving the stem of his wine glass around in his fingers.

"Unless she was kidnapped. Or killed."

Standt took a small sip of the tangy wine. If he gulped the glass full down he was going to fall asleep in the chair, which wouldn't have been a bad option if Amanda's case wasn't so compelling and conflicted with contradictory theories.

"What makes you think that she was kidnapped?"

This seemed like a wishful theory, like Crenshaw's, presupposing that Amanda was still alive.

Wilcox's eyes flashed when he turned back to Standt. "Because the present theory is horseshit. Killed by a shark…" He scoffed. "…Drowned. In the first case, the paddleboard doesn't show that evidence. Shark attacks are extremely rare, especially during the day. She wasn't doing anything stupid–like swimming in murky water at sundown.

"In the second case, Amanda was an extremely strong swimmer. An athlete. She'd been on a paddleboard for years. The bay was not dangerous that day. It was actually placid.

"And of course, God forbid, her body was never found. They never found my daughter. They wiped their hands of this case. The so-called chief of police here; a clown. He's more interested in getting sauced. A total incompetent!"

Wilcox was talking faster, in a hoarse voice, the anger and frustration mounting.

"I have all the information for you right here. I've been keeping track. The paper on top has the name and number of the Kauai policeman who investigated the case. The second contact is a local investigator, a man named Chris Ke' alohilani. I suggest you talk to him first. He's willing to explore different options. He can answer specific questions about the island."

"I want to look at the evidence," Standt said.

Fatigued, his eyes cast over the empty sea and the cloud-roiled horizon. "The paddleboard."

"That's all there is, for evidence." Wilcox finished his wine. Cleared his throat.

"Time is of the essence, detective."

"I understand. A few more questions though."

"Anything."

"Who were Amanda's friends here?"

"I don't know, precisely. She worked for a group…"

"Pure Food World."

"So you know that. They are anti-GMO activists. A pressure group. So she worked with some local activists, scientists."

"Do you happen to know whether she had a boyfriend, or boyfriends, here?" Standt hated asking that question. He understood what Wilcox was going through. But they were too essential to ignore.

Sam didn't seem to mind.

"She never shared much of anything of her private life with me. Never had to. I knew she was committed to her work. She was too serious at this point in her life to take boys…they were distractions as far as I know. She thought the world, its flaws and its victims, were more important than romance."

"I met Dash Crenshaw."

"You did."

"He seems pretty broken up."

"I don't think Amanda took him very seriously, or as seriously as he *thought* she did. He wasn't out here, until recently."

"He might disagree with you. He said they weren't seeing other people. He also disputes the official explanation of what happened."

Wilcox bristled below the otherwise courtly and

controlled surface. "Anyone with half a brain wouldn't believe a word of this cockamamie investigation."

Then he shifted gears, indicating that he found Crenshaw, the thought of him, vexing. Possibly Sam and Dash had some friction.

"She could have done anything she wanted to. She would have made a crack litigation attorney. She was…is…brilliant. And…" He acted like he couldn't go on.

Standt turned away, got up from his chair, and walked over to the edge of the bluff. He wanted to give the old lawyer some space, for his private grief. He admired the sea. Far below the bluff, the sun reflected hotly off the calm ocean's surface, as if water could singe and burn.

A tiny lone stick figure maneuvered their paddleboard over the reef, making the very picture of solitude.

"Can you take me to where Amanda was last seen?" Standt said to the sea. "The St. Regis?"

"Now?"

"Yes."

"Of course." Then Wilcox stood up, as if to leave. For the first time Standt noticed how tall his rail thinness made him seem, a height that lent him prestige.

"Before we go," Wilcox said. "I want to give you something else." He went back into the residence for a moment and came back with an iPad, which he handed to Standt.

"You can use this while you're here…I've loaded it with a video of Amanda that you should watch. A speech and panel discussion.

"You shouldn't try to look for someone until you know them. As much as you can from this. You probably want to change. I'll show you your room. You sure you don't want to crash for a while before we go over to the beach?"

"No, I'm fine. I will change my clothes though."

Standt went into his room and changed into shorts, a t-shirt, and a rubbery pair of sandals, then he and Wilcox drove over to the St. Regis, which was only about two miles away.

CHAPTER 9: HANALEI BAY

They valet parked at the entrance to the Regis, then they took a long flight of stairs down to the beach. The stairs wound down steeply through a bamboo grove and the steps were covered with crushed, wild unripe bananas.

The bamboo leaned and creaked in the trade winds, making a sound like a distressed, haunted bird. The sound gave the scene an antiquated, imperial ambiance, like colonial Dutch Java.

When they hit the sand, Wilcox removed his sandals. Standt did the same. It felt good to walk on warm, finely grained white sand. They walked past a beach cabana with formally dressed waiters and tan hostesses busily serving the early cocktail crowd. Then they passed a counter where people were renting snorkeling equipment, sea kayaks, and paddleboards.

Wilcox gestured toward this small sea-sports operation. "That's where Amanda rented the paddleboard."

More gear, which Wilcox had referred to as SUPs (stand-up paddleboards), were racked up on the beach nearby.

Standt couldn't help but stare at the women lying on the chaise lounges and sunbathing on the posh beach, with their glistening bodies and spare bikinis.

Given the lack of any tall structures on Kauai, the St. Regis wrapped itself grandiosely around the small peninsula on Hanalei Bay. It seemed excessively big and imposing. At the foot of the hotel lay the posh beach scene.

The two men walked through the sand along the lapping water toward Hanalei Town, and the resort gave way to a local scene of surfers, swimmers, and paddlers.

A lineup of surfers caught the waves on top of the reef a ways out from the coast. A river flowed from the ocean into what to Standt looked like a Southeast Asian jungle with flowers floating down the waterway. Some of the paddleboarders drifted serenely along Hanalei Bay, their paddles raking the water with a leisurely rhythm.

The bay had a gentle swell, compared with the flat river. The people disappeared down the river, around a corner of brown, sandy beach, coconut palms, and thick tangled vegetation.

The lush green hillsides rose swiftly from the sunlit bay into immovable, dark gray clouds that hid the mountaintops. The view was beautiful and forbidding; you didn't want to venture into those mountains without a guide; maybe never.

Wilcox had on a pair of aviator sunglasses and was staring out at the water. He was still looking for Amanda, waiting for her to show up.

"This is where Amanda left on her paddleboard that afternoon."

"I have to say," Standt said. "These waters do not seem dangerous at all."

"Yes," Wilcox said. Then he pointed along the sea, tracing a pattern from the river to the surfers. "She would just take a loop here. Maybe come back in an hour. That's what the rental people over there told me."

"Where was the board found, eventually?"

Wilcox pointed in the opposite direction, around a corner from the languid St. Regis beach scene.

"Sealodge Beach. On the other side of that peninsula, a fisherman found the board washed up on the rocks the following morning."

"Wait," Standt said. "If she headed that way…"–he pointed toward the entrance to the river from the bay–"then how could she end up on the opposite side of the bay, over there on Sealodge?"

The current seemed to be going from the bay into the river, but it probably led in different directions, depending on the beach a paddler or kayaker left from. It *was* Hawaii, which is known for its strong, unpredictable rip tides and currents.

Wilcox looked back at Standt meaningfully. "I don't know why her board ended up over there."

"What did *they* tell you?"

"They claim she paddled in that direction from the beginning, changed her usual route. They claimed she probably attempted to go around this peninsula and enter the adjoining bay, which is just beneath our bluff in Princeville."

"But no one saw her do that?"

"No. I gather she took her normal route. That's the way she was, a person who loved their routine. Like me, her dad."

He looked down at the sand. They were still standing by the water. Standt thought, as he had before, that it was odd and counterintuitive that Amanda's body had not been found.

The ocean did not look dynamic here, in the summer.

When people fell or were dumped into the Hudson River in New York, which has a pretty strong current, their bodies were found more often than not. Usually within twenty-four hours.

The bay was calm, like it was now, during the week Amanda disappeared. It was clear, with a mellow, small swell, and shallow above the reef for several yards. Why would the board wash up and not her body, if she drowned?

There were many divers and snorkelers off the St. Regis. Why didn't they find her body? Standt was assaulted by questions, which he mostly handled silently.

Wilcox idly checked messages on his cell phone. He seemed exhausted. A woman strolled through the sand past them in a bikini. She'd left nothing to the imagination and gave off an air of diffidence and lassitude.

She seemed American–with dashes in her pedigree of French, Italian, maybe Columbian or Puerto Rican. Standt watched her sashay past him. She was a knockout, totally in command of her temporary sector of beach. She did a short loop on the beach, then angled back to a chaise lounge, stretched out her slim, darkly tanned legs, and turned her face away from the sun.

Then a waiter strolled over, smiled, and took another order.

It seemed a lifestyle that Standt wouldn't mind living for, well, about a year. Yet if he let up now, Amanda's mystery would remain just that, a cold case. Another unsolved crime in the tropics. She'd end up like Ashley Hedgeland, and that made his gut clinch, as if at the world's never-ending perversity.

Wilcox stood on the edge of the water with his hands in his pockets, looking sad and dejected.

"Sam."

"Yeah," he said, as though Standt had interrupted

another reverie.

"I think I'm finished here, for now."

"What are you going to do?"

"I'm going to talk to Chris…"

"…Ke' alohilani. Right, you'll never remember that name. But he seems to know what he's talking about."

They walked back up the beach and reached the bottom of the long flight of stairs. They bent over to wipe the sand off their feet and put their shoes back on. Wilcox gazed at the bay once more, then back to the detective. He stood up straight.

"Detective?"

"Yeah?"

"We don't have much time. We have to pull out all the stops."

"I'll do everything I can."

"In the event this was foul play, what's happened to my daughter…" His chin faintly quivered. "I want them annihilated. We will show no mercy."

That was an utterance right out of New York, not Kauai.

"All I can do is find suspects. Perps. The legal end, the outcome, I have to leave that up to judges and juries." It hadn't always ended up so cleanly in Standt's old cases. Some men won't let their prosecution get to a judge. They don't want to be caught alive.

They quietly climbed the stairs, then Sam let Standt drive his car back to the condo, while he left for his room at the St. Regis.

CHAPTER 10: CARLA

Upstairs was the locally famous, or infamous, depending on who you were, St. Regis terrace. It was a place to be seen, or be broken. A kind of high-society stage, and a trust-funder's favorite drinking hole, with a view to die for. Carla Holloway was a waitress on the terrace. It seemed like she was always working, racing around the lazy, hedonistic crowds with her drink trays.

Carla knew Amanda Wilcox. She hadn't talked to anybody about her disappearance. She'd kept it inside, out of fear and mourning. She'd always looked up to Amanda. She didn't think she could hold all this stuff inside of herself forever.

Amanda hung out on the terrace. She was the kind of naturally eloquent woman Carla thought she could never be. And she was always kind to Carla. She tipped her generously and never had airs.

That's why Carla was bothered, haunted, by the things

she'd seen on the St. Regis terrace leading up to Amanda's disappearance. She didn't tell anyone about them right away, because they seemed par for the course for the crowd at the St. Regis patio bar.

But now she brooded over them, to the point where the thoughts bothered her late at night and kept her up. It was something she would normally shrug off once her shift was over, three people having an intense tete a tete. A few voices raised.

She'd count her checks, collect her tips, and go home to Hanalei Town and have a smoke and a few glasses of wine, usually a few too many.

But it means something when the person disappears afterwards. She felt like she knew Amanda, who had a familiarity with Carla that bordered on kinship.

# # #

Carla served Amanda coffee once on the patio. That was one of the first times Carla had met her. Amanda was not fashionably dressed that time; she had on faded jeans and a loose shirt, which still showed off her willowy and lithe body. All she wore on her feet were sandals, which she removed when she sat on the couch.

Amanda was alone on the terrace. It was late afternoon. She seemed contemplative, almost melancholy. Carla had seen her sometimes with people at the St. Regis–now Amanda seemed to be enjoying a rare moment of solitude, as if regretting the time she had expended socializing and chatting away the brilliant afternoons above Hanalei Bay.

Carla wanted to strike up a conversation, but not impede upon Amanda's privacy. So she waited for Amanda to break the ice.

She asked where Carla was from. Connecticut, just above New York City, so that shared history led to the things they liked about New York; the Natural History Museum (they both liked dinosaurs), farmer's markets in the Village or Union Square, skating in Central Park, and seeing a star on stage (Carla had seen Al Pacino, for Amanda it was Vanessa Redgrave).

Amanda didn't even mention that Turner Espray was her friend; she didn't brag or put on airs with Carla.

Amanda curled up on a couch that they had on the terrace and it was as if she and Carla were friends chatting away in an apartment. Carla loved how smooth and tan the tops of Amanda's feet were.

"I love your hair," Amanda said, and that comment made Carla feel warm all over.

"How long are you going to be on Kauai?" Carla asked. She'd love to be able to do something with Amanda, just the two of them, go shopping in Hanalei Town or paddleboarding. But she didn't dare ask.

"Probably another month," Amanda said. Carla was finding things to do around the patio, like wipe down tables, so she could just hang out with Amanda.

"Do you have a boyfriend?" Amanda asked, out of the blue. Now the conversation was turning to real girl-to-girl confiding in each other.

Carla shrugged. "Not really."

She'd had a series of unsatisfying one-night stands, usually with guys who worked at the hotel. She didn't have time for a boyfriend, anyways. She kept wiping down a nearby table.

"You?"

Amanda shook her head. "Men," she said resignedly. It seemed to be a sweeping comment that questioned the worth of the entire universe of males. Carla sensed Amanda's weariness with romance. She'd had her pick of men.

"What do they want, really? Sex? They want attention,

that's what it is. They want the same kind of attention their mothers used to give them. It's a craving, a constant search for the doting woman they lost when they grew up. They need to be praised. Needy, needy, needy."

Carla set down a tray she'd been carrying and put her hands on her hips.

"I know what you mean. I know a guy one night, and he already wants me to start cleaning up after him. Do his laundry. Clean up his bedroom."

"Ain't that the way it is?" Amanda said, smiling at the mischievously shared grievance. "Find a nice guy, smart. Please God, look down upon Carla and me and bestow upon us the nice man. Find us someone who isn't just trying to replace his mother. Do you think we ever will Carla, find someone like that?"

Carla said, "Yes. But I'm not sure they're here on Kauai…this island attracts a certain kind of guy. Not sure if they're your cup of tea. You do some serious work here. Really heroic, on the GMO stuff."

"I'm no hero," Amanda said. "Far from it." Then she looked away to the bay, which reflected the sun beams striking through the torn shreds of clouds on the mountains.

"You ever had problems, you know, with addiction?" she said abruptly.

"Yes," Carla said, after she got over her surprise. She jumped on another opportunity to confide. "I did some weird stuff in high school. Eight years ago. I had an eating disorder. I cut myself. Imagine that, I did harm to myself. Sometimes I think I don't know that person."

"What's the trick? To dealing with your problems?" That was startling. Amanda was asking for *her* advice? Carla couldn't believe it.

"Stay busy. And have good friends, family members, that can keep you on track. Always have someone around…you can talk to."

Carla wondered what Amanda's addiction was, but she wasn't going to ask. Whatever it was, it couldn't be too serious. Amanda was outwardly beautiful. The way she carried herself…like a relaxed queen–but royalty with a common touch.

"I hope you find someone soon," Amanda said, after a pause. A warm breeze blew in from the mountainside, up from the river. They both looked away thoughtfully and admired the way the sun played on the bay, their own shared moment uncluttered by men.

"I hope he's a nice man. Because you're a really nice person Carla."

"You too."

Carla remembered that conversation oh so vividly, because of what happened the last time Carla had seen Amanda on the patio. Amanda was in a drastically different mood then. She was with a guy Carla thought she had seen before, but didn't know by name.

Carla wanted to tell someone about that last time on the terrace, badly. But she didn't know who to go to. The memory was eating her alive.

CHAPTER 11: WATCHING AMANDA

Standt returned from the St. Regis beach to the condo on the bluff, then executed a complete face plant on the bed. The room had brown wooden louvers on the window. An overhead fan provided a slight breeze. Standt shut the louvers that cast stripes of sunlight on the bed and floor. Then he collapsed.

When he woke up he had left drool on the pillow and he heard a crowing rooster, even though it was not early morning. The roosters on Kauai didn't seem to know the proper time to crow. The island was full of wild chickens, presumably liberated from coops by Hurricane Aniki in 1992.

Wilcox's people had left all kinds of food and drink in the refrigerator for the detective. He ate a sliced papaya and a couple of hard-boiled eggs, standing quietly by a counter looking out at palm trees swaying in the early-evening trade winds. Then he sat down in the living room to view Amanda's video.

He noticed the sun was setting, so he stepped outside onto the bluff to watch the sublime effect of the waning rays against the ocean and the steep cliffs. A dark-gray cloud the shape of an anvil sailed across the horizon. The light-blue sea was flecked with thousands of the tiny white frothy waves.

Still emerging from the cobwebs of his nap, he shook his head at the paradisiacal view. Watching the sunset, and recalling the demure beach babe who'd earlier walked past him beneath the St. Regis…*The lives some people lead.*

Then he fetched a cold water from the refrigerator and sat down to review the video on the iPad.

Amanda stood at a podium. She had long, dirty blond hair that fell down over a black shirt with no collar. She wore a string of small pearls and some other kind of necklace with a pendant hanging from it. He wondered what the pendant contained.

She was tall, with the narrow, fine features of a leading lady.

But it was Amanda's voice in the video that gripped him; its timbre, the life-force it conveyed. She spoke quickly, eagerly, as though there would never be time enough to get all the important words out. Her voice, her thought flows, were avid. You wanted to listen to her. She was erudite and clearly enunciated, without an accent but with a sense that she was engaged and passionate about what she was saying.

Wilcox was, of course, correct. She had a crackling intelligence, not pedantic, but likable. He could imagine her swimming, or on her paddleboard.

His instincts told hi her disappearance was something other than an accident.

The world, at least how he had experienced it as a Manhattan detective, was so epically fucked up that the Amandas in life often turned out to be the predators' main targets.

On the video, she was talking about the GMO food industry. The feverish corporate drive for profits, the non-existent regulations and oversight, the hazards of introducing new untested DNA into the food supply.

People have enough problems with gluten, wheat toxins, pesticide residues, and the like. Now we were adding more "xenophobes" to the food supply, so a few corporate VPs could get richer.

Hawaii was being used as a guinea pig.

Take back your food freedom. Cede control back to small farms and Mother Nature; use natural pest control.

Amanda was willful, her eyes flashed out at the camera. You wanted to believe her; follow along in her passionate wake.

Standt's heart went out to Amanda. It had been what? Nearly two weeks since her disappearance? She must have ruffled some serious corporate feathers.

He was going to get ahold of this local cop Chris and see what he had to say.

CHAPTER 12: KE'ALOHILANI

Chris Ke' alohilani lived on the south shore of Kauai, near the resort center of Poipu. He was a local cop, a felony investigator, which usually involved car and high-end condo break-ins and violent brawls among local surfer and skateboarder gangs, but he also taught surfing.

At this moment, he was on Sam Wilcox's payroll. As Wilcox had explained to Standt, Chris didn't buy the local theory for Amanda's disappearance. He thought it was bullshit. He had his own theory, but Wilcox definitely wanted him to work closely with Standt.

They agreed to meet in Hanalei Town at a place called The Dolphin Center. It was a place where you could eat outside on the river.

Standt drove his rental down there the next morning and parked outside the restaurant, where he found Chris sitting on a stool outside.

Chris had long black hair with gray streaks tied up in a

pony tail. He had white, thigh-length shorts, muscular calves, and sandals; his purple t-shirt read Nukumoi Surf Shop. He looked like he had just been surfing followed by a quick change, probably because he had.

The Hawaiian, originally from the Big Island, had a warm smile and Kon Tiki style tattoos imprinted on each of his calves. It was one of the first times Standt had actually liked the look of tattoos. At home, these "decorations" made most of the young people look like they were just out of prison, or on their way in.

Typically, in America, the first thing they will do to reform or reclaim a gangbanger is have their tattoos removed. Here, it was Polynesian versus Sing Sing art.

Chris had a goatee to go with the pony tail, his bushy black mustache drooping over an ingratiating smile.

"You can call me K, or Chris," he said. "Most visitors can't pronounce my last name."

"I'd like to try. I mean, my name ends in 'dt,' so most people don't get that." Standt took a seat on a stool next to Chris.

Standt didn't want to be known as another ugly American type, coming over to the islands for a whiz-bang debauch at the local Luau, a long weekend acting like a douche, then leaving the tropical idyll with not much more than a maxed out credit card and a hangover.

Arriving only with an endorsement from Wilcox, he wanted to earn a little cred from the locals.

"Okay. Ke' alohilani."

Standt gave a decent shot at its pronunciation. K smiled. "Not bad."

"What does it mean?"

"Heavenly sky. A mythical place in the heavens, in Hawaii mythology."

"That's nice."

"It's Hawaii, it's Kauai. The sun will always shine on you. If it's raining, just wait. We live here in a happy state, it's a kind of heaven for visitors. The real thing. Come here, relax, let the good mojo come to the surface."

"Yes, I can see that."

"Except for Amanda." K's face went impassive and serious, like a cloud passing over the sun. Awful things happen in paradise, too.

"Really tragic, what happened," he continued on. "I was hoping she was only lost."

"So you think she's dead?"

"What else? If she's alive, kept somewhere, there's no ransom letter."

"No body either."

Chris shrugged. "It's been known to happen. A drowning. It's a big ocean."

"How many people drown on Kauai each year?"

"A couple dozen, on average. Mostly tourists; they get drunk then go swimming in the waves at night or dive off a boat."

"How many of their bodies *aren't* found?"

"Not too many."

Standt shifted his attention to the crux of the matter. "What do *you* think happened to Amanda?"

Chris crossed his arms sitting on his stool, but before he spoke a waitress came by to take their order. Standt ordered a halibut sandwich, Chris K the ono sushi. Nearby, the river crept through mangroves, appearing like heavy floodwaters. It carried a flotilla of flowers and lilies.

Chris wasn't going to tell Standt his precise theory right away. It seemed like he wanted to keep it suspenseful.

"I have pictures of the paddleboard. I assume you want to see them."

"Yeah." He got them out, laid them on the table next

to the water glasses.

Standt got out his glasses and looked at the images of the board from different angles. They looked, to him, like a surfboard lying on the beach, banged up with gouges sliced out of it, like it had been caught in a machine.

He noticed a cable or leash lying next to it.

"You know for a fact that this was Amanda's?"

"Yes. She rented it. It has a serial number. Greg told me about those."

"Who's he?"

"The haole who runs the sports shop at the St. Regis."

"What's an haole?"

Chris laughed. "A caucasian, a white guy, like you. Not a Hawaiian, or Polynesian."

"Gee, somehow that doesn't sound like a compliment."

"It's not bad. It's just a word." Then he turned his attention back to the pictures.

He pointed at certain places on the board. "Those aren't shark bites, or anything like them. A shark will bite the board, but the bite is in the shape of a shark's mouth or jawline, and you will usually find a tooth in it."

Standt pulled one of the pictures closer to him.

Chris went on, "Someone tried to make it look like a shark bite, maybe by using an actual tooth to mark up the board, like here…" He pointed to scrape marks on the paddleboard. "It's a crude attempt, really. Pathetic. Inauthentic. The rest of the marks…probably made by a machete."

"A machete? Why?"

Chris shrugged again. "They're really trying to make the board look damaged and thrashed up, but they failed. Grade F. I saw it right away."

"Who would use a machete here?" Chris's conclusions about a faked crime were beginning to make sense.

"Anyone could have a machete. We do have fruit and coffee plantations here."

"Ever seen anything like this before? Like the m.o. of a previous crime?"

"No."

"Who took this picture?"

"Bruno Reilly."

"Who's that?"

"He's the sheriff in Hanalei. He had jurisdiction."

"And he gave this to you?" Their food arrived. Standt was starved; Chris seemed hungry too. Their discussion commenced around big bites of delicious seafood. The Dolphin Center was filling up. Chris smiled and waved at several people who came in and took tables.

Skinny, tan women with sun-bleached hair and loose casual clothes; unshaven men, some middle-aged, who looked like they'd arrived in Kauai when the Beach Boys first made records, then never left.

One of the people was a young, lean, very tan, dark-complected man who lay his short, wide surfboard down outside before he came into the restaurant.

Chris gave him the smiling, two-fingered "Aloha" sign.

Standt looked at the kid's surfboard. "That seems much smaller than the one in the picture."

"Surfboards, except for beginner's longboards, are shorter and lighter than paddleboards. They both come in all shapes and sizes. Basically the SUPs are bigger. The longer they are the faster they go. Some people race with them."

"So this guy Reilly, you say he gave up the photo without a fight?"

Chris K took a bemused glance at two older tourists edgily moving their SUPs down the river. He had a warm, laid-back confidence. "Let's just say I owe him a favor now."

"He believes this shark or drowning theory."

"He came up with it, with his people. They were called in when Amanda's SUP was found. The shit hit the fan with the media. You know. They waited about twenty-four hours, then when no one found Amanda, they came up with this cockamamie story."

"If no one really believes it, if the investigation has no credibility, then why stick with it?" Standt had taken part in many a hairball investigation, with heartbreaking female victims, in the city, but even New York with its turbulent social and political complexities, had a way of filtering out the bullshit and getting to the heart of the matter.

"I'd believe in drowning, if it didn't seem like the board was doctored. She was killed, and they put her body somewhere. They want us to believe she was swept out to sea, or bitten by a shark."

Chris took a deep swallow, looked down, and tapped on the table. In a way, he was a smart guy with the wrong job; he liked surfing, and mellow atmospheres. He wanted to be outside under the sun testing himself with the other young hombres. Investigating dead people was anything but.

"Did you bring this up with the sheriff? That the image looks fishy? Pardon the expression…"

The surfer smiled again. He had a Zen quality. Standt already liked working with him. He trusted him.

"No."

"Why?"

"Because he would have denied it. You can't come up with your own theories, about deaths or homicides, because it riles things up. People on the island just want to resolve issues. Move on. Let the sun back out. They're afraid…"

"Of what?"

"Creating bad press. Uptight mojo. Stormy oceans and murders scare away the tourists. This is a happy place. A happy place that needs visitors. Lots of happy ones." Chris understood both the reality of its beauty, and the marketing of Kauai.

"By the way, Bruno Reilly comes from back your way."

"New York?"

"No, Boston. He used to be a Boston cop. Moved out here, took the sheriff job in Hanalei Town five years ago."

Standt thought he might have recognized the name.

"Do you know why he came out here? Other than the obvious reasons, the sea and the sand?"

"No. Why?"

"Because there was a guy named Reilly who got involved with a scandal. The shooting of a young black man…it might be him."

"I don't know anything about that."

The image of Amanda's paddleboard, sitting on the table surrounded by food plates, was printed out on paper, but still of good photographic quality.

"Do you have a digital version of that?"

"No." Standt would have it scanned in then give it to Church. The hacker would blow it up by a magnitude of about one hundred. Then they would really analyze it.

"You're 100 percent sure it's Amanda's?"

"99 percent sure."

"Okay." So Standt wouldn't have to seize the board as evidence and have it scraped for Amanda's DNA, but he might have it analyzed for someone else's.

He was curious about that black cable in the picture. He pointed at it.

"What's that?"

"The leash. It's attached at the ankle."

"So you don't lose your board…"

"Yes."

"Isn't it strange though, that the leash came loose at some point? Aren't they securely attached?"

"Yeah. They don't come off that much. Never for me. It's a couple of loops around your ankle of Velcro, and mine's never come off. It is strange…I noticed that too. If she had been knocked off her board in some way, her board would have remained attached by the leash. It's safer; you can always grab your board for flotation if you get in trouble."

"I assume there's no damage to the leash, like a tear?"

"No."

"So what do you think?"

"Whoever killed…snatched her, removed the leash from her ankle. There's no other explanation. If she got hurt or injured in the water, the leash would have stayed on. She wasn't in any big waves."

"How do you know?"

"Because Hanalei doesn't have any big swells right now." He looked to the river, squinting in the sun's reflection, as if its placid current could be any indication of the swell height at the source of its water, the bay.

"Did you get a chance to dust the board, and the leash, for prints?"

"It's clean. They probably wiped it clean."

The waitress came with their bill, took away the plates. They each paid.

"Can I have this?" Standt said, pointing to the print.

"Yeah sure. Where are you going now?"

"I don't know. Go see Bruno Reilly."

"You won't see him."

"Why?"

"He makes himself unavailable. You have to make an appointment. Probably tomorrow."

"What? I thought he was the sheriff."

"He's quirky. Doesn't like to take orders. Or be bothered. Kind of a mystery guy. Maybe that's why he came to Hawaii, so he could be that way. The best way to see him is to say you'll buy him a drink."

After leaving money for the lunch, they got up and walked over to the river's edge.

"It's one of the places where Amanda liked to paddleboard," Chris said after a moment's pause. They both stared at the river, with its southeast Asian or Javan textures, the floating blossoms.

Standt had to cover a few more angles.

"Have you had an uptick of crimes against women lately?"

"No."

"Do you have any cold cases, involving disappearances?"

"No, very few."

"Tell me honestly. Who do you think took Amanda? You know the people on this island. You've seen what they're capable of, what happens around here. What's your gut telling you?"

Chris K seemed private, and proud; the first air of defensiveness crept into their encounter. He didn't like to be pinned down, by this stranger. He took a deep breath.

"You got most of my theory. The ideas. Her drowning or shark attack was faked."

"I know. But why? What's the rest of it?"

Chris looked around as though someone was listening. As if that rich, green, suffocating overgrowth of tropical vegetation that was almost everywhere on Kauai was hiding one or more pairs of listening ears.

He almost whispered. "Somehow, she got into something that some very bad guys wanted to stay hidden. They plucked her off the ocean. They were watching her." He had a burning, unblinking look Standt hadn't noticed before.

"No one saw it. She's dead. We won't find the body any time soon. You asked for my gut feeling. You got it. Do you want to see where we found Amanda's board? It's very near where you're staying."

"Yeah."

He wanted to contact Bruno Reilly, and scan in the evidence, get it to Church.

Church was back in Manhattan, but Standt had a feeling he was going to need him here in Kauai. He wanted to look at Amanda's credit card and checking-account records for the last few weeks.

Standt and Chris walked back to their cars in the restaurant parking lot. Standt was hot. The sun was always there, baking the back of his neck, where there would always be a glistening layer of sweat. They drove the few miles back up to Princeville to take a look at Sealodge Beach, where the paddleboard was found.

Oddly, for a laid-back, slow-paced place like Kauai, he'd almost wrapped up his first day investigating on the island, yet Standt felt things were already moving too fast for him.

CHAPTER 13: THE GLORIES OF POT

Standt was groggy and jet-lagged, six hours off his own New York time zone. He completely passed out again after leaving Chris in the parking lot of the Sealodge units. It was late afternoon.

They'd walked back from Sealodge Beach up a steep footpath that was slick with red mud in places and came through dense vegetation, where a few wild chickens poked around in the dead leaves. Fruit trees and giant weeds overhung the trail.

The white beach, a tiny half-moon in front of the reef, was secluded and beautiful. The mangled board was found on some black rocks on the edge of the beach. Only one person was there now, a scraggly, bearded barefoot guy who looked shipwrecked but who was actually a shell jeweler. He was scanning for his raw materials at the edge of the water.

The beach was located far around the corner from a

peninsula that is adjacent to the St. Regis and the bay. Standt bought Chris' view of a faked ocean accident, but they had no suspects. That was the hole in the surfer's theory. He had a scenario that made sense, a gut feeling based on the evidence, but no human faces to connect with it.

They'd both concluded that the perps probably brought the doctored board by boat and planted it in the rocks, knowing that the small beach was often vacant.

It was conceivable that Amanda had paddled around the corner from the bay, but that direction was against the prevailing current, which tended toward the Hanalei River and Beach (the opposite direction), and was also a deviation from her usual inclination to paddle out to the bay. Or down the river toward The Dolphin Center.

After Chris left, Standt passed out again in the room with the wooden louvers, then woke up at some indeterminate time in the dark. He made himself coffee, then went outside and looked at the bright stars of Hawaii.

The only thing that had taken him aback at the beach was that Chris had lit up some weed. They were standing on the beach, no one else around, and Chris had removed from his top pocket what was virtually a cigar.

With the nonchalance of unwrapping a stick of chewing gum, he lit the tip of the doob with a lighter, brought it to his lips, and inhaled deeply.

Standt still loved the aroma, but couldn't let himself indulge. Chris held the weed out for Standt, with a sidelong glance at the detective, who shook his head. It was awfully tempting to take a toke with a premier mellow dude such as Chris, and the tropical context befitted an improvement in one's mentality and perspective: warm waves curling in amidst the gentle trade winds and setting sun. No one else around.

Chris looked at him and then both his eyes and smile

appeared to be laughing. He exhaled with a guffaw.

"Relax detective. We're on to this case. We can take a short break. This is Polynesia."

Standt could feel the change come over him, even though he hadn't toked. *This was Polynesia*, not some frenzied Midtown police precinct jammed with sweating, stressed, and neurotic cops.

Chris' merry eyes turned back to the ocean, where he appeared to be looking at the distant flat horizon and the burning alteration of colors, his smiling gaze traveling over it and sensing permutations Standt couldn't detect.

Chris took another toke. "I don't like smoking alone," he said. "I don't like it."

The trade winds moved the palms with a gentle rustle and the bent-over trees made an iconic image with the blue sky and orange-fringed clouds.

I didn't tell you to take the thing out and light it, Standt thought to himself.

The lit weed smelled rich and aromatic, the sun, a fiery disk half submerged in water. The rippled surface of the ocean reflected the sinking sun. Standt pinched the thick joint in three of his fingers and drew it towards his mouth. He'd made the decision. He inhaled.

"That's what I'm talking about!" Chris laughed. His smile was handsome and knowing. Then Standt handed it back to K, holding in the smoke, which he let out with a few convulsive coughs.

"My man," Chris said, patting Standt on the back. The water was coming in over their feet, and Standt focused on that warm wet feeling, wriggling his toes in the fine sand. He took another toke, then looked about, paranoid.

"No one cares," Chris said dismissively. "We'd tell them it was medical, if they were uptight." Then he looked around and he added, "No one's here."

The ocean was engulfed in flames. He and K had consumed another day on Kauai, Standt's second.

Standt didn't remember being so relaxed, at peace with the world. He took another toke, returned it to the care of Chris. He stared at the way the sunlight reflected off a sheen covering the black volcanic rocks on the edge of the beach; he studied the frothy sea surface for dorsal fins, whale's flukes, and Bottlenose dolphins.

He took another draw off the short, thick joint, now burned about halfway down its original length. Quietly, and with a glib ease, he began to solve some of the world's problems: poverty, despair, war-mongering; the inadequate distribution of resources.

He moved his feet around on the moist sand. He felt fine. The sun and the trade winds stroked his skin. But he told himself to smoke no more. Still serene, he was however disappointed in himself.

"I'm going to teach you to surf," Chris said, to no one in particular. "That's the next thing you have to do on Kauai."

Standt stared at the sea some more, and tried to picture a beautiful woman with long blond hair, a sea nymph, dipping her paddle into the gentle swell. She raked the water behind her with a graceful stroke. She had a calm rhythm, as though half-flying along the top of the water, long legs in a tight swimmer's bathing suit. Goddess-like.

CHAPTER 14: KATIE

Not soon after Standt awoke with his face crushed into a pillow, he heard that Katie Hudson was arriving in Lihue the next day. She was doing the feature story on Amanda for *Slate.*

Standt had stayed stoned for hours, and the pot gave him strange dreams when he slept.

He met Katie at the airport late the next morning, then they returned to the Princeville condo so she could freshen up. Meanwhile, Standt was trying to get an interview with Bruno Reilly. True to Chris K's description, Reilly seemed to keep himself out of touch.

By mid-afternoon, Standt still hadn't heard from the sheriff, but Katie wanted to head to the St. Regis patio bar. It wasn't just to be briefed on the Wilcox case. She wanted to soak in the view and sip an icy glass of Pinot Grigio.

She wanted to get her feet wet in Kauai, literally by a short walk down the posh beach.

At the St. Regis, they took a couch in the open air of the terrace. The sun still blazed, yet it hadn't illuminated enough of Amanda's fate for Standt's liking.

"My word," Katie said. She was admiring the high mountains, with their clouded summits, and the lime green slopes that dipped steeply into fields of long grass, and then Hanalei Town and the bay. "That *is* beautiful."

Bruno Reilly had finally returned an email message to Standt, saying he'd meet the detective and Katie at the St. Regis. Reilly probably figured he could filch a couple of rounds off the detective at a bar he otherwise couldn't afford.

Standt had also sent an email to Church telling him to download (and try to condense) everything he could find on Amanda from the last year, including forum conversations and tabloid fodder. Then Standt would sift through the archival material to see if anything jumped out at him. He needed a suspect.

# # #

It was hot on the terrace. They almost had the place to themselves. Katie sipped from a big-bellied goblet of white wine, the color of honey with the heat beading the glass with droplets. She took a long drink and a welcome breeze came up and mussed up her hair. Standt thought she looked tired, but terrific and relaxed.

He thought he was falling in love with her. She had dark auburn hair that fell below her shoulders and a beige summer dress with narrow straps, showing off her dancer's physique. She crossed her legs; she had wonderful muscular calves. She winked at him.

"I want to get a tan here!" she declared. She was getting pretty tipsy. Then she put on a pair of dark sunglasses, leaned forward, and looked around again.

She peered with wonder at the cloud-cloaked

mountains.

"Those mountains look scary," she said.

"They are. They don't get climbed."

"Who lives there? King Kong?"

"No one, as far as I know. Biologists, conservationists go there."

Standt was nursing a cold Sauvignon Blanc. Compared with Katie, he felt like an expert on Kauai. Maybe it was because he had gotten stoned there. He'd never live that down with Church, after what they'd gone through together with rehab.

Of course, Church would probably never find out that Standt had toked up on the beach–Standt didn't even plan to tell Katie, he was so embarrassed by the episode.

But his indulgence, while not unpleasant, left him feeling like a hypocrite.

He sensed the sluggishness of the dope as a residue from the day before. It peeled away from his consciousness strand by strand.

A busy, friendly waitress came by with welcome ice waters.

"Hey guys, I hope you didn't think that I forgot about you!" She had a slim build, long, brownish blond hair, and an off-white St. Regis uniform. She seemed a little harried by her resort job, but she wasn't letting it get her down.

"No one else is on the terrace because it's too hot," she said. Katie ordered another glass of wine; Standt passed on the next round.

"This is the most beautiful view I've ever seen," Katie murmured. "And just us…"

"That will change when the sun goes down," the waitress, whose name was Carla, said. "The people will pour in. You see, the building blocks the trade winds right now. It's hot as Hell…pardon my French. It would be breezy otherwise."

"I like the privacy now," Standt said. "Thanks a lot for the wine."

"No worries. Come here for the winter some time. The waves on Hanalei Bay get so big, they have tow-in surfing. This is the primo spot for watching it."

"That's hard to believe–it's so quiet now." Then Standt saw an opening with Carla.

"Do you know Amanda Wilcox?"

Carla seemed to abruptly shift into a lower gear. "Yeah. It's horrible," she said. "It's terrible that they haven't found her."

She bent down and started wiping a nearby table distractedly.

"She ever come in here? To hang out?"

"Yeah," Carla said, almost shiftily. "She came to the St. Regis. A few times."

"Who was she with? Anyone familiar? I'm just curious."

He was trying to keep it light; later, he planned to interview Carla as an investigator.

"She came here with other women, usually. Once alone. She came with a guy once."

"Who was *he*?"

"I don't know," she said dismissively. "Do you guys want any food?" She wanted to change the subject.

"No. By the way, how did you know this woman was Amanda Wilcox? I mean, before she disappeared and got into all the papers?"

Carla moved closer to him, so other people wouldn't hear. They were almost the only people on the patio anyways.

"You know, sir…"

"Karl."

"Okay, Karl, it's pretty cliquey around Hanalei, the St.

Regis. Everyone knows everyone, almost. There's a lot of gossip, a lot of social life. Money flows around, influence. Snobbery. The whole ball of wax."

Standt was smiling, because he liked Carla's candor and he had her on a little roll. "What were they saying about Amanda? What was the scuttlebutt?"

"She was a really terrific-looking gal, with personality. You couldn't *not* notice her." Then Carla seemed to pause and obsess over something.

"I've got to go–check on something in the kitchen."

"No, who was she with, really? Can you tell me?"

"No one I know."

Standt was fumbling for a card and his old NYPD detective's badge.

Katie was sitting quietly, sipping her wine, enjoying the sun, and looking amused. She'd witnessed Standt's investigatory banter before.

Carla paused and sat on the arm of their couch with a towel in her hand. She was thinking of that guy she saw Amanda with. He plagued her; the memory. She'd never seen either of them again.

"There are a lot of trust-fund types here. They mostly live up at Princeville, or in the nicer sections of Hanalei Town. Some of them are trouble. They always get what they want, that's the problem, while the rest of us are working two, three jobs."

"And Amanda was with some of these guys?"

"Maybe…"

"Do the Monsanto people ever come up here?"

"Sometimes. Probably. Don't really know 'em."

"Let me give you my card," Standt said. "I'd like to interview you some more. I'm sorry. I'm a Manhattan investigator. I'm actually trying to help find her. Can you write the number down, like for your cell, so I can reach you later?"

She picked the card up and looked at it, then she scrawled her number on the card and set it on the table.

People suddenly poured onto the terrace. Another beautiful sunset unfolded over the water. A formally dressed wedding party stopped in with a photographer; they took pictures briskly and left.

Carla disappeared out the terrace entrance. Standt put the card in the breast pocket of his shirt.

He felt like a bit of an interloper with the swanky crowd that was filling the patio bar. Like he used to feel at his ex-wife Lara's fancy fundraisers at the The Russian Tea Room in Manhattan.

Katie was still smiling beatifically at the Hanalei Bay panorama; her happiness and glow had some of Chris K's high voltage. Then she sighed.

"Well, I should get back to work I guess…what's new with the Amanda case? What's going on now, have you found out anything?"

"Her death probably wasn't an accident, if you can call that new."

She looked temporarily sober, and got out a notepad.

"How do you know that?"

"Not yet." Standt gave a little "settle down" sign with his palms facing downward.

"You mean the notes?"

"Yeah. I'll tell you everything you need to know for your story, but let's keep it undocumented for the time being."

She shrugged, took another sip of the wine, and crossed her legs. She had a sandal that dangled off the tips of her toes and bobbed up and down with her preoccupation. "Suit yourself. But honestly, what do you think happened to her? You can speculate, right?" The question, it seemed, the whole world wanted to know.

"When are you going to run this story in *Slate*, anyways?"

"Maybe in a week, ten days."

"I don't want whoever's done this to have a clue where I'm looking."

She watched him impassively. "So she was murdered?"

"Off the record, okay?"

"Of course. I wouldn't blow your cover, baby. Does a week or ten days give you enough time?"

Standt scratched his head. "Yeah. Wilcox is going to be mighty disappointed if I haven't cracked this case by then."

"What makes you think this wasn't an accident?"

"Because the paddleboard they found is doctored."

"Doctored? Really?" Katie chewed on the back of her pen. She put the pen down and took another sip of her wine.

"They found it around the corner from that point down there, you know." He gestured to the beach beneath the terrace bar, and its nearby peninsula.

The wine had made him sleepy. He wondered when Reilly would show up, if ever. They called it *Hawaii time*, here, the propensity to be late. It could end up driving him crazy by the end of the week.

He flagged over a waiter and asked for an ice coffee to perk himself up. Katie looked away to the Pacific Ocean, in the direction Standt had pointed, then turned back to him.

"Manhattan is still going nuts over Amanda. The mayor mentioned her in a press conference. Lots of stuff is coming out, tabloid junk that may be untrue, about her nightlife. The media is still milking the story. Parties, boyfriends, drugs. Most of it, possibly, untrue."

"What kind of drugs?"

"You know, tabloid garbage. Lots of drinking and Ecstasy and cocaine."

"Really?" He couldn't picture that, at all. It was a completely different image of Amanda than he had in his head. He hoped Sam Wilcox, who clearly adored his daughter, hadn't heard about this. He wondered if she did it with Crenshaw.

"What's the evidence of the partying? She seemed, to me, really intellectual. More of a philosophical, activist type."

"There is none. It's pure paparazzi-style hearsay."

The waiter flew by and left an iced coffee, which Standt picked up and sipped. He kept his voice low.

"My guy here, Chris K, thinks she's dead. It will be hard to find the body. He thinks she stumbled on to something someone was hiding, like a drug operation. They got rid of her. But he has no suspects."

Katie looked off to the North Pacific in a ruminative fashion. "Maybe she decided to lose herself, to get away from the attention. The living in a fish bowl. She wanted to escape."

"The local yokel Bruno Reilly is meeting us here."

"Now *that* will be interesting."

Just then a man with a fancy white suit wheeled on to the patio with a Champagne cart. Everyone in the bar stopped what they were doing and watched him. He was an older man who reminded Standt of the suave guy with the salt-and-pepper beard in the Bacardi Rum ads.

The man took a Champagne bottle in one hand, and gripped a small silver sword in the other. He explained how at the St. Regis, they have an every-6:30 p.m. ritual, at sundown. When the sun sets, he attempts to cut the Champagne cork off with the sword.

Sure enough, the first swipe sliced off the top of the cork, as the warm sea in the foreground of the Napali Coast was awash in hot hues of orange and red. Dark silhouettes of palm trees gently nodded toward the water.

Standt thought of the "wine-colored sea" from *The Odyssey*. It was another idyllic day's end on Kauai.

Just that moment, as the suave guy pushed the cart away and the crowd applauded him and dispersed, Bruno Reilly swaggered onto the patio.

CHAPTER 15: BRUNO REILLY

Standt knew he'd heard about him before. He'd seen the press photos; read the stories. It was the Jaylen Kinsley case; a young unarmed black man shot three times in a dark foyer in the Dorchester projects. Bruno Reilly was the cop. The rumors and accusations made the light of day; the hair-trigger temper and the heavy boozing. He was raked over the coals and suspended, but not prosecuted. No witnesses.

All this came to mind as Reilly strode up to their table. He was about about six foot two, with thick sunburned forearms, a surfing t-shirt, and shaggy, graying hair stuffed into a Red Sox hat. He looked like he was recently off the plane from Logan, but not much like a uniformed cop anymore.

Standt knew it was him, by the old story and his appearance, the way a cop's career can work you over. He waved Reilly over.

Bruno awkwardly weaved through the cocktail crowd,

shook Standt's hand gruffly, then took a seat on the couches across from the detective and Katie.

"Ah," he exclaimed, impressed by the surroundings and settling into the cushions. "I don't get the chance to come up here that often. We haven't met," he added, looking at Katie directly.

"Katie Hudson…" He gave her a brief, wolfish scan, and they lightly shook hands.

He took his Red Sox hat off in the heat, betraying a bald crown. He had the flushed look of a drinker, but otherwise didn't seem older than about forty-five.

Immediately he jerked his hand in the air, summoning a waiter. The man who was working with Carla looked up, seemed to get a disappointed look upon recognizing Reilly, and came over.

"Chivas, on the rocks," Bruno said curtly. His reputation precedes him, Standt thought.

"Pardon if I put on some sunglasses," Bruno said, leaning back in his chair. Standt had the impression that the shades were there to permit Reilly to leer unbidden at Katie.

"So…you two are from?"

"New York," Standt said. the scotch arrived, and Bruno took a greedy gulp of it, the ice cubes tumbling down the steep angle of the glass and crashing on to his upper lip. He put the glass down.

"Welcome to Kauai. Best island in Hawaii, by far. The Maui coast is all condos now; you can still sleep on the beach here. Not that you guys need to do that…hanging out at the St. Regis. That would be slumming it, for sure. What can I do for you?"

"Amanda Wilcox."

"Surprise, surprise. You're working for her dad, Sam?"

"Yeah."

Bruno paused a moment and seemed to size Standt up.

"So you worked the streets in the old days?"

"Yeah."

"Where?"

"Manhattan, Midtown. The Detective Bureau, at the end. You?"

"Boston, Back Bay. South End. I never go there anymore. Hawaii's my beat. The weather's better. How long you on the island?" He reached over and snatched the scotch again, as though he was afraid someone else was going to drink it.

"As long as it takes."

"Well, I can recommend some good restaurants, and you should go fishing, take the heli tour."

"I'm not touristing. I'm trying to find Amanda Wilcox."

Bruno looked borderline patronizing. "I doubt you've had many cases like this in the city…"

"You'd be surprised."

"So you're Wilcox's man now, huh?"

"I am."

"Because of that, I'm here. But I don't know how much I can help. We're near to closing the case."

"Really?" Katy said, incredulously. "It doesn't seem the case is closed to me. No one's found her, or evidence of her…"

"We have our theories. And just give it some time. What do you do?" Bruno couldn't hide another once-over her body through the dark lenses.

"I write for *Slate*."

"Never heard of it."

"Its an online magazine. We're covering Amanda's disappearance."

Bruno shook his head, gulped down the last of the diluted scotch. "The story that won't go away…" His hand went up to signal the waiter for another scotch. Then he sat back in the couch heavily. "Tragically…"

Standt couldn't tell whether the remark meant her disappearance was tragic, or Bruno simply found the intensified attention everyone paid to the case to be a tragic burden he had to bear.

"I need to know what your evidence is," Standt said. "I want to look at what you've got, so far."

"Forensically?"

"Yeah, forensics. And who are the primary suspects?"

"There are no suspects in an accidental death," Reilly said matter-of-factly. "She was killed by a shark. In all likelihood."

He told the story like he had told it four hundred times before, and the tone suggested that he didn't believe in it anymore. Maybe never did. He spoke quickly, by rote.

"The paddleboard had bite marks all over it. Tear marks, like a thrashing shark. Terrible to think about."

"Did you find a tooth?"

"No tooth."

"Did you have a shark guy look at it, a biologist?"

"Yeah, she's at the University of Hawaii. I'll give you her cell phone number. Email, whatever."

"Did you pursue any other angles, such as any men close to her?"

Reilly flared at Standt under the surface.

"Who you been talking to, Chris?"

"Chris K, yeah. We spoke yesterday." We actually got high together, Standt thought to himself.

"That's what I thought. Chris is a good guy, but in this case, he's talking out of the side of his mouth. He has a big imagination. And he likes to smoke the funny stuff a lot.

You get that here in Hawaii, fun in the sun. Goofy stuff under the sun.

"People don't go out on paddleboards and get mugged here. They get swept out to sea, drowned, smashed by a big wave, or sometimes, attacked by sharks. Don't go out in the ocean myself. Gives me the creeps."

"Yet you moved to Hawaii?"

The waiter brought his third scotch glass, which he gazed at warmly as it was placed next to him. "I like the lifestyle better. The weather, the food, the booze…the women." He took off the sunglasses and winked.

Standt could all but sense Katie's disgusted grimace.

"What did Chris say, exactly?" He put the tinted glasses back on. "Never mind, I could guess. The shark attack was faked. That's his favorite story."

"You work with him a lot?"

"Yeah. It's a small island, population-wise."

Then he seemed to move on from Chris.

"As I said, we found no evidence of foul play. We don't have very much crime here in Kauai. Only about a dozen, sometimes twenty, people drown per year. Amazing given the thousands of people who are in the water every day. It's paradise compared with…New York."

Katie leaned forward. "…Or Boston."

Reilly laughed in a phlegmy way. The scotch was doing it to his throat. The heat of Kauai that never went away.

"Or Boston," he repeated. "How's your story going? Here in Hawaii, people wouldn't mind a little closure on it, as a matter of fact."

"Isn't it a little soon for closure?" Standt said. "We don't have a clue what's happened to her."

"Shit happens," Reilly said, and it came out sounding pissy and callous. Then he leaned back in his chair and came back to them with a more conciliatory tone.

"I wish I could give you something new but…she was really popular on the island. No one would have wanted to hurt this young lady. She wouldn't have hurt a fly. I see no motivation, like a jealous ex-husband, a random, unprovoked attack. That stuff happens here, but only in the other neighborhoods."

"Kauai has bad neighborhoods?"

"A few. You know, like low-income housing. But…about Amanda, it's just tragic. The ocean is a vast, wild kingdom. Easy to get into trouble in it. People relax, get complacent, then get dead. Sometimes it's easy to forget that."

Standt seemed to remember Chris saying something like that, but even the surfer didn't believe for a moment that the Pacific Ocean and Mother Nature were the true suspects in this case.

Reilly swished the ice cubes around in the bottom of his glass; he seemed to ponder Amanda by staring down at the leftover scotch.

"What about the GMO protests?" Katie said. "That's a pretty intense issue on Kauai. Could perhaps a pro-GMO person, like a farmer with a grudge, have gone over the edge? Done something to her? Someone from Monsanto?"

Bruno bristled again under the surface. His face took on a deeper shade of red. "No. I mean, between you and I, it's mostly corporate types supporting the GMO. Those guys don't jump into a cigar boat at night and go off someone on a paddleboard. It's not their style; their modus operandi."

"That sounds more like drug dealers," Standt said.

"We have those, but it 'aint Miami here. That's for sure."

"What's the biggest drug problem on Kauai?" Cops who smoke weed with surfers, he thought to himself guiltily.

Reilly hesitated, as though not wanting to say anything bad about Kauai.

"Meth amphetamines, probably. The kids have found Ecstasy, that's for sure. It's not a massive drug problem here. Not like the cities…Amanda, those anti-GMO protesters, they weren't into any of that. She kept her nose clean, as far as our investigation went. I never heard any stories…"

Bruno did no more, in Standt's mind, than put up roadblocks.

"What are your informants saying?"

"Informants? Like I said before, this is Kauai, not Bedford Stuyvesant…"

"There are no utopias," Standt said, laying it out there like an aphorism, a platitude that couldn't be challenged. He'd seen vicious crimes committed everywhere, no matter how nice the place was: Dubai and Switzerland. Every investigator needed informants.

"Okay, informants," Bruno said, somewhat impatiently. "You're looking at them, all these yuppies here at the St. Regis."

There was a certain truth to that. Standt had to pry open the St. Regis social scene. He could use Carla the waitress for that.

"Can I see Amanda's paddleboard?"

Reilly shrugged, as though tired, exhausted finally, of everything Wilcox-related. He ran his hands over his face and hair. He seemed ready to wipe the slate of her.

"Sure, just drop me a line before you come." He looked down at his now empty scotch glass.

"This is on us," Standt said, reluctantly, gesturing to the glass. Paying for Bruno's drinks seemed like an immutable, universal principle, like the sun always setting over the western horizon.

The light was low over the patio, where torchlights

had come on. It was romantic, like old Polynesia. A beautiful breeze blew up from the bay.

"I gotta go," Bruno said, standing up with his tall, slightly stooped and crooked bulk. "Nice meeting you."

Standt stood up and shook hands with him, saying "I'll be in touch." Katie didn't say anything, then Bruno half smiled at her and staggered through the crowded patio and left.

"That was useless," Katie said, edgily. "What do you think his schtick is?"

"Collecting an extra paycheck," Standt said. "Running a blocking maneuver, so he can stay on the payroll."

"Whose?"

"I'll find out."

CHAPTER 16: THE LAST TIME SHE SAW AMANDA

Carla thought of that man again, now that she had the detective's card. Not that the guy on the terrace with Amanda was ever very far from her mind.

He was a type who hung out at the St. Regis. He was tall, slim, with a constant disheveled Sunday-morning look, as if he had gotten dressed in his preppy clothes that he'd just plucked off the floor, where they had been flung in a heap the night before.

The guy never had to look put together or neat, because he didn't have to impress anyone, or look responsible. He was independently wealthy, and unshaven.

They sat together and ordered drinks, Amanda a glass of wine, he a bourbon on the rocks. She said a few things to him, with a serious face, then turned away as he talked. Carla wasn't waiting on them. She was glad, for once, because

Amanda was in a different mood and didn't seem to be having a good time.

It was like she was there against her will.

Carla invented an excuse to get closer to the conversation, so she aimed for a tray another waiter hadn't gotten to yet. She drifted closer to Amanda and the man. She didn't like him. She knew that right away. He had an air of entitlement, the way he draped his long legs and wrinkled khaki pants over the chair in front of him, the way he swilled his drink with his head back listening to Amanda, then leaned forward arrogantly to make his own points.

His gestures were designed to remind Amanda that he was in charge.

She'd seen too many guys like this at the St. Regis. They wore untailored but expensive clothes and drank heavily and stood off to the side to sneak cigarettes where they weren't allowed. They were the dregs of the trust-fund crowd that parked temporarily in Kauai.

Amanda didn't acknowledge Carla, which also made her concerned. She wanted to ask, "Is there anything wrong Amanda?" But it just didn't seem the right time to do that.

She got close to the two and she heard Amanda say testily, "Did you actually believe I would do that in the first place?"

"Why not?" the man said. "It's what you want, isn't it?"

Amanda shook her head angrily, then she had a look that said to Carla, "Why am I even here? What have I done to myself?"

Then another unsavory character walked on to the patio, a woman. The man waved her over. Amanda shifted uncomfortably in her seat.

The woman was short, sun-burned, and scraggly looking, with an air of homelessness and abandonment. She had a jean skirt on and jailhouse tattoos on one of her forearms. When she came out on to the terrace she looked around in wonder, then caught the eye of the two people waiting for her.

She had a gap-toothed smile on one side of her face, and she seemed to leave a trail of stale cigarette smoke as she walked across the patio and took a chair.

The man, tapping on the table impatiently, stood up when the woman came to their table. The woman sat down but he remained standing. He said something to her and the woman pushed a small brown-paper bag to the man. Carla was watching them intently.

Amanda had her eyes averted, toward the bay. She looked under-slept. The man in turn pushed the bag and its contents to Amanda, who took the bag after a pause, and only reluctantly. Then everyone waited without saying anything.

Carla really wondered what was going on. What were these people doing with Amanda? But she had to leave and take an order on the other end of the patio. She took the order and looked up and saw the lady laughing, cackling, and Amanda had a look like she was about to start crying.

The man aimed a dismissive wave at the woman. He reached into his pocket and seemed to hand her a bankroll.

As the woman was leaving, Amanda got up too and was about to walk away when the man grabbed her forcefully by the elbow.

"Let go of me!" she said. This time Carla didn't hesitate. She walked over to the table, and passing the scraggly woman Carla heard "Good luck with those two sweetheart."

"Is there anything wrong?" Carla asked.

Amanda looked simmering. The man still had her by the elbow.

"Nothing. Nothing at all," he said.

Amanda was looking at the floor, then looked up and said, "I'm okay." Then she talked down her nose to the man. "I can speak for myself, thanks."

Still tugging her by the elbow, the man led her to the exit. She ripped her arm away and flashed a look behind her, but it wasn't one that sought help.

"Are you sure?" Carla called out to her.

Amanda turned away, miffed, angered, and embarrassed about who she was with. She just left, expressionlessly. That was the last time Carla saw her.

CHAPTER 17: DOWNTIME

Standt could feel the evening breeze through the louvered window. He lay on his back on the bed. Katie got up and slipped out of the room. The stars were bright and the palms swayed in the trade winds that buffeted the dark bluff.

Katie re-entered the bedroom and dropped a short summer nightgown to the floor. She stepped out of it delicately, as a shy young woman would step from a pond. She leaned back and shook her hair out. Standt couldn't take his eyes off her body, light brown skin and voluptuous and luminous in the pale light.

Silently, she scooted into the bed next to him. The light through the window shifted around their nude bodies as thick leaves rustled in front of the moon. All he could hear was the the cacophony of cicadas. The ceiling fan creaked and rotated unseen in the dark.

Then she was on top of him. He was hard and ready. She put him inside of her and rotated her hips and made a "mmm" sound. Her brown hair, untied, fell over her shoulders and partially covered her breasts, which stood out prominently as he caressed their undersides and moved his fingertips over her wide, brown nipples. She moved her hips as if the bed rocked in a gentle ocean swell.

It had been a long day for both of them, and they'd drunk a lot of wine. They were tired but with plenty of left-over physical desire. They didn't have to say anything; nothing was left to do but screw. It was just going to happen, without delay or forethought, the way things always bend toward the erotic in the tropics.

They hadn't been going out that long and weren't living together, but they made love like experts. As if they knew exactly what the other person wanted, at just the right moment.

They fell asleep next to each other in a tangle of sheets, their legs entwined, the ceiling fan rotating like a squeaky wheel. Standt could hear the cicadas in the trees and feel the breeze from the fan. As he dozed off, he imagined the darkness and the wind rustling and shaking the palms.

# # #

They awoke the next morning, a little too early. Standt got out of bed and made coffee. A few minutes later Katie drifted in dressed in a white bathrobe. He gave her a cup; she left and came back in summer clothes. Then they drank the coffee together sitting out on patio chairs in the grass.

"I could marry this woman," Standt thought, even though Katie sat tightly with her legs crossed and seemed to pensively sip her coffee.

By this point, He was afraid of running into Sam Wilcox.

He was living high on the hog in Kauai, and had even

gotten stoned. He was having a fine time with his girlfriend. Wilcox was going to think Amanda was a meal ticket, a low priority for Standt.

Somehow, on Kauai, he hadn't been able to keep himself from slipping a degree into self-indulgence. It was all part of the island's ambiance.

Cops were not highly paid, given their extreme job demands. As sheriff of Hanalei Town, Bruno had to be no different, even though the placid beaches were far from Boston's urban streets. The temptations were always there to take bribes from people who wanted to feel less guilty, which can usually be accomplished by you looking the other way.

Standt also recalled that the Kinsley family had launched a civil suit against the City of Boston and Bruno. A lawyer's fees may have taken a bite from his limited finances, if not decimated them.

Taking a look at Bruno Reilly's bank account would be revealing. He had the feeling that Bruno seemed to be dragging his heels on purpose and for a profit.

CHAPTER 18: INCONCLUSIVE EVIDENCE

It turned out that Kauai had a lot of banks. This was where Church came in. Sure, it was quasi-legal to have him hack into customer records to find Bruno's money trail.

But moving slowly and not cutting corners or using the best technology was of no help to Sam Wilcox or his daughter.

Wasn't the NSA's capturing of millions of emails and phone calls a "quasi-legal" activity at best? Not that Standt wanted to use the federal government's own excesses as an excuse for his own, but he did want to find the missing person.

Standt was on the phone with Church the day before, giving him the information on Bruno. Then, as early as he could the next morning, following coffee with Katie, he and Chris K visited Hanalei Town's evidence room, down the hill from Princeville.

It turned out Bruno wasn't home. He kept banker's hours. But a deputy let them into the room, which was a messy storage area with the mangled paddleboard leaning up in the shadows of a grimy corner.

Any biochemical evidence of value on the board was certainly long gone (and never collected in the first place), including DNA and fingerprints. The board was contaminated by whomever was moving it around in the room, and it had been sitting in salt water for an unspecified period.

He wiped it for fingerprints and blood samples anyways. There probably were none; and the deputy was useless, since he wasn't there when the board was found and appeared ignorant of the case's details.

Bruno had said they hadn't found any bloodstains on the board.

Even to a non-surfer's untrained eyes, the paddleboard looked like it had been assaulted by a frenzied, machete-wielding human. It was hacked at rather than bitten and shook by powerful jaws.

Standt took pictures of the board from every angle, then he emailed the digital versions to Church. The hacker would go over them with a fine-toothed comb, otherwise known as Photoshop. Then he and Chris returned the board to the feckless deputy and left.

Standt figured that Church would have something on Bruno's bank accounts soon. He usually didn't take too long to penetrate a bank's defenses, using his laptop arsenal in a small Brooklyn apartment.

Sure enough, when Standt returned to the Princeville condo, he had received a bunch of messages from Church. They contained the information from Bruno's personal account at the Central Pacific Bank. Standt sat down on the couch to look them over.

As Sheriff, Bruno had the expected direct-deposit payments each month by the town office of Hanalei.

However, several very strange entries popped up on a monthly basis for the last six months. He had electronic payments totaling nearly $65,000 from an entity called De Reuterstad Group, LLC.

One of the payments was for $12,750, and all of the entries were in the ballpark of $8,000.

The payments exceeded Bruno's sheriff salary, by far. Standt fired off an email ordering Church to gather background on the De Reuterstad Group. Later in the morning, Standt took a call on his cell phone from Sam Wilcox.

It was the beginning of his fourth day in Kauai, and he still didn't have any solid leads, only hunches and Bruno-related suspicions.

"Detective, I wanted to touch base with you before I left Kauai. I'm going to come back soon, but I have some business to attend to in New York. You're my point man now in Kauai. I'm counting on you. Have you found out anything on Amanda?"

Standt wished he had something more solid to relay to Sam.

"Yes, but I'd rather not tell it directly to you over the phone. I did want to ask you whether I could have direct access to Amanda's last week of phone and credit-card records. I need to know everywhere she went, when, and who she was with before her disappearance."

"Of course, anything you need. I have power of attorney for my daughter and I will release all those records. You will receive a secure overnight package of those documents at my Princeville residence. Please keep me informed about what you find out over the next twenty-four hours."

Standt was just grasping at threads right now, hoping to find one that he could weave into a coherent narrative.

"I will. You can count on it. I'll be in touch."

He felt guilty about not accomplishing much more on Kauai than raising suspicions about Bruno, which would be the natural reaction anyways from anyone who met him for the first time.

Why did Standt have to go and get stoned with Chris?

# # #

Church's research had turned up a connection between De Reuterstad and Monsanto, which had bought the Dutch agricultural science company two years before.

So Reilly was doing some shady work on the side for a Monsanto proxy. He was "investigating" Amanda's disappearance, but at the same time there was intense friction between Amanda's organization and a giant corporation that planned to make billions off of GMO.

There was an obvious conflict of interest, but no concrete evidence, such as a thread of email messages. Maybe that would come later.

Standt called Chris K at about 1:30 p.m. on his cell phone. Katie was still off on her excursion taking photos for *Slate*. He caught the casual surfer at yet another mellow, Zen moment.

"Bruno is on the take with a Monsanto subsidiary."

"You don't say? Good old Bruno. How much?"

"Over one hundred grand a year."

"Wow. Good cash." Chris paused. He and Bruno had a history. The gears were turning. "How do you know that?"

"We got into his bank records. What do you think he's doing for them?"

"Ten to one they'll say it's for security, for their

parties. You want to ask them? They're all at a party tonight. There's a fundraiser at the Princeville Golf Club. Monsanto has a big entourage there. You'll probably see Bruno's ugly mug at the front door. A ticket will set you way back though."

"I can get Sam to cover that." And he could too. Standt didn't think Sam Wilcox was going to question his expense reports like the Midtown precinct used to.

Standt looked at his watch; just late afternoon. Plenty of time to wander over to see what was cooking at the golf club. He didn't know yet how he was going to confront Bruno, except he knew it would be pretty direct, possibly ugly.

Bruno was making more money from the re-seeders of Hawaii than he was executing his so-called sworn duty as sheriff.

"You said Monsanto had a large entourage," he said to Chris. "Who am I looking for?"

"They have a fat cat VP named Ted Rand. He runs everything for Monsanto on Kauai. Spends most of his time on the yacht and the golf course. He'll be there with his slutty wife Betsy."

Standt couldn't help but laugh. Chris K was actually getting worked up.

"He uses a conservative Hawaii paper to write bullshit editorials about how the GMO industry is so good for the islands. People write letters firing back; he's had death threats. It gets heated. He's hired body guards, the Samoans, but he doesn't hide. He shows up at the biggest parties, fundraisers.

"They give to good causes to sugar over the raping of Kauai. I see he and his wife around town, getting in and out of their chauffeured Mercedes.

"He actually lives on the yacht offshore most of the time. If you go, just ask one of the waiters who Ted Rand is."

"You want to go with me? Free ticket…"

"No man. I'm going to hit the sack. I'm a little tuckered." It was not yet two p.m.…

"I've been surfing all day–had a late one last night."

Then Chris added: "What are you doing tomorrow?"

"Don't know yet. It depends on what I find out tonight. Why?"

"I've got a friend who can give you the best, cheapest tour of Kauai. He's a helicopter pilot. He had some clients cancel on him. He's going to give me a ride to…Come with me. You can get an entire overlook of the island."

He sounded sleepy, as if already signing off for the day.

"It will give you a whole new perspective on Amanda. We can see the complete route she took on her board that day. Kauai, it was her Queendom. She's out there, somewhere, dead or alive…good luck man. I'll call you."

"Wait, when's the fundraiser?"

"Starts at six…"

"Okay, thanks."

Standt dived into his luggage and pulled out a few things he could wear to the golf club. It was, at any rate, within walking distance, so he was going to take the stroll.

He didn't know whether Katie was coming with him. That might be easier, as it would make his presence there less suspicious and more like a fancy date he was treating his girlfriend with.

When he came out of his bedroom in a pair of plaid shorts, sandals, and a tennis shirt, his cell phone rang from the table beside a sliding glass door. He answered it and stood by the screen looking out at the Pacific Ocean.

He heard Church's muffled voice. Standt was surprised, because they were usually email and text-message only.

"I thought you might want to know this."

Church sounded like he was talking with socks in his mouth.

"Okay."

"I found an inscription on the paddleboard image. You said let you know right away if I found new evidence. I don't know whether you know this already but, the board was rented at a place called Samba Surf & Sport."

"Okay." Standt was thinking "So what?"

"That's different than that hotel place…"

"The St. Regis."

"Right. You thought the girl rented the board at the beach."

"Okay, thanks for telling me, but what's the significance? There must be a lot of places to rent paddleboards. Maybe she got a better deal…"

"So I went and I checked out the Samba place. It's owned by a guy named Brad Manley."

Church was actually getting pretty good at pursuing new angles, rather than just accumulating reams of data without interpretation. He could unravel investigatory threads from new information. He was less mechanical than he was in the past.

"Who's he?"

"Just nobody. A surf shop owner. But I did a couple of searches on him, and he has a brother."

So do I, Standt thought. Church was talking like he was sucking on marbles.

"Named Doug…"

"Speak up, okay?"

"I gotta go soon. Anyways, you should know that the brother got caught growing tons of hashish on the island. Wasn't Amanda Wilcox, I mean, dealing with farms issues and GMO?"

"Good. Primo. There could be something there. Can you email me the links?"

"Yeah."

"You keeping your nose clean?"

"What do you mean?"

"You're not doing any Ecstasy?"

"Not since…"

"Okay, keep it that way." Now if only Standt could keep his own nose clean.

CHAPTER 19: THE GOLF CLUB

Standt did a little reading on Church's new angle using his laptop. He thought he'd fill his mind with new information before making his way to the Princeville Golf Club.

Doug Manley wasn't a penny ante drug dealer. Three years ago he was caught trying to move hundreds of pounds of hashish and cocaine into Hawaii from Mexico. He was prosecuted by the feds and did a year and a half of time in the Federal Detention Center in Honolulu.

Standt checked the web site for Samba Surf & Sport, but there was only a little profile of Brad Manley, the owner.

The Manleys apparently grew up on Kauai surfing and were well known around town. Brad did a little competitive surfing and apparently had the oldest surf shop on the island. But the web site wasn't about to grace its pages with Brad's deadbeat brother Doug, the drug felon.

Doug seemed to think he could make a lot of easy

money outside of surfing. He came back to Kauai from the Honolulu detention center, but still couldn't stay out of trouble.

As part of the package, Church had emailed Standt a link to another article in the local newspaper, *The Garden Island.* It described a recent "altercation" and arrest outside of a bar in Kapaa, a town on Kauai.

A man accused Doug Manley of stealing $800 from him without handing over some "prescription medication" that was part of the transaction. They'd had a brawl in the parking lot; Manley had brandished a knife during the fight. He was arrested again, charged with aggravated assault, and would be arraigned soon.

Doug was a badass and seemed to miss out on the mellow surfer's chromosomes that his brother was born with.

Standt read more of *The Garden Island* story. The assaulted man accused Doug Manley of growing a large stash of hashish and other narcotics crops on Kauai. He was shifting from exporter to cultivator.

But Manley's lawyer called this accusation, which was made during questioning and then to the press, "unsubstantiated hearsay and nonsense."

The article identified Doug Manley as an employee of Samba Surf & Sport, which of course carried no mention of him on its web pages.

So Amanda had stumbled into a paddleboard rental place that employed a two-time loser and a thug. This told Standt nothing new about her disappearance. Just like the lawyer said, the link was "pure hearsay."

It *was* suspicious that the shop had failed to reclaim the paddleboard, and that apparently they weren't questioned by Bruno at all. Very strange, an oversight that was so obvious that it had to be on purpose.

Standt saved the web links and kept the squalid small-time local episode at the front of his mind.

He got ready to go to the golf club. Katie had told him to not wait for her; she was driving back from a distant town called Waimea. It's not that the Kauai towns were all that far apart, but the island had traffic issues and relatively low speed limits. She didn't know whether she would return in time, or really have the energy to go hang out at a party.

Then again, whatever was going on at the Princeville Golf Club would probably be good for her story. She said she'd try to meet him out in front of the club.

Standt left the condo and walked about a mile through the balmy darkness of Kamehameha Road, lit only by its quiet, well-kept suburban bungalows. The evening trade winds rustled the thick green tropical vegetation and palm fronds that grew past the roofs of the homes.

The outgrowth grew up the sides and over the roofs of the homes, giving parts of the neighborhood an airless, claustrophobic aura.

He turned left on to Ka Haku Road, and found the golf club in a few blocks. The party was a brightly lit and loud island of activity. Cheesy ukelele music played under bright spotlights. The sprawling, lit-up club house was setback from the perfectly manicured greens.

SUVs and luxury cars pulled up out front and disgorged their passengers, wearing party and formal-golf attire. One by one the cars cruised up to the entrance, then were whisked away by valet parking.

Standt didn't have a ticket yet, but he had a wallet full of cash and figured he could buy a ticket at the door.

There had to be at least forty people milling around out front, some sipping from fluted Champagne glasses. It was already a big party.

Standt hoped he could simply confront Ted Rand or Bruno outside and dispense with the party itself, but they were nowhere to be found.

He didn't know what Rand looked like anyways, so when he bought his two tickets at a booth out front, he asked the lady if Ted Rand was already in the party.

"Yes," she said bluntly, as though it was common knowledge. "Have a nice time."

Another lady at the front door smiled and draped a lei of yellow blossoms around his neck. The party was a luau, and folksy Hawaiian music played from speakers mounted alongside a spotlit fountain.

Standt would text Katie about her ticket if she could get there on time. He hoped she could, if only for the reason that the tickets cost $125 each. If Standt couldn't nail down Rand and Bruno at the party, he was going to have to eat the $250 himself.

He grabbed a handful of shrimp inside–he hadn't eaten recently–but avoided the alcohol. There were several bars dispensing free drinks. The party room had long linen-draped tables laden with roast pig, stir-fried veggies, local fruit, and lavish desserts. Plenty of opportunity to pig out on pig, even though the majority of men, mostly middle-aged or elderly, already had the evidence of numerous prior luaus spilling over their distended waistlines.

More than a hundred people milled around with their multi-colored dresses and leis, their golden, leathery tans, the dyed hair and surgically augmented bodies and designer watches and opulent jewelry. It decidedly was not a surfer's crowd, nor did it have the placid beach vibe.

It was corporate, affluent, a Fox News and Orange County, California type gang pining for the halcyon days of Ronald Reagan.

# # #

The only awkwardly dressed person other than

himself was Bruno, who was off to the side of the fray taking part in a rapid two-handed consumption of hors d'oeuvres. Before he approached Reilly, Standt took a waiter aside and asked him if he could point out Ted Rand in the crowd.

Rand was standing with a group of people chatting and drinking wine. So here was Kauai's supposed Big Cheese. He didn't appear particularly distinguished. Medium height, white golf pants, aviator glasses perched above his forehead, a Hawaiian shirt with the buttons undone on top to reveal a little graying chest hair.

From top to bottom, he looked the part of a Monsanto apparatchik: tanned skin, thinning white hair, and a pair of alligator skin cowboy boots.

Standt fingered his old NYPD detective's badge. He kept it around to help with the introductions. The badge was no longer officially sanctioned; it was a relic that was still however an essential part of his identity.

He knew he wasn't supposed to use it; the badge was retired. The truth was, however, he *was* on an official investigation, only this one was private.

The detective took a gulp of his ice water and walked over to Rand, who had broken free from his crowd of peeps for the moment. Standt was just going to throw out the payments to Bruno as one would toss a stone into a placid lake, to see where the pattern of ripples would take him.

He removed his badge and walked over to Rand, who stood with his wife holding on to his drink and surveying the crowd with a dazed, authoritative benevolence.

Standt stood next to him and couldn't avoid the awkwardness.

"Excuse me sir, you're Ted Rand?"

"Yes." Rand had a glassy look, as though he wasn't really acknowledging Standt, who might have been an expendable thought passing through the executive's mind.

"My name's Karl Standt. I'm investigating the Amanda Wilcox case."

This got Rand's attention, but by only a few degrees beyond apathy.

"You are, are you? Found anything?"

"Her? No. Can you tell me anything about her disappearance?"

"Me? What would I know?" Now he blinked and fixed Standt with an inquisitive stare.

"You and Bruno Reilly might have some information I would find valuable."

"What are you doing at this party? What was your name again?"

"Karl Standt." He flashed Rand his badge. "NYPD, former detective."

"Former. What did they do? Kick you out?"

Now Betsy Rand, who stood beside Ted with a drink in her hand, had fixed Standt with a curious stare.

"Who are you working for? Now?" she said.

"Sam Wilcox, Amanda's father."

She looked at him thoughtfully then held out her hand and introduced herself. She had a purple-flowered dress, low cut, and a curvaceous figure that he immediately latched his attention on to.

She fit the bill for one of the rich local phonies, but there was something genuine about her, more penetrating.

"Why do you want to talk to my husband?"

Ted Rand sipped his wine and, viewing Standt as an irritant he had no time for, let his wife do the talking. He wanted to party and get buzzed.

"I'll cut to the chase," Standt said. "I've had a meeting with Bruno Reilly."

"Yes, Sheriff Reilly," Betsy said, as though correcting him.

"He has a theory about Amanda's disappearance, which for some reason no one believes is true. He won't budge from it. But he has no solid evidence; a very weak case. You're locals, I take it. You know Reilly."

Standt didn't dignify the officer with "Sheriff," which was a huge slight if the Rands were savvy about how detectives normally address other policemen.

"Why do you think he clings to a discredited theory about Amanda's disappearance?"

"Why do you care? About what we think?" Betsy asked. They both had latched on to Standt with stares, Betsy's slightly less glassy and hostile than Ted's.

"Why think the young lady, Amanda, didn't drown?" Ted asked rhetorically. "Or was killed by a shark, god forbid?"

"Because the evidence is weak," Standt said. He didn't want to go into too much detail. The Rands didn't have to know this. "I suspect tampering, possibly a cover-up."

Ted Rand stepped back away from Standt and was actively looking through the crowd, then he raised his hand and began signaling someone. Betsy still regarded Standt with rekindled interest.

"Again, why bring it up here, with us?"

"Because Monsanto has Bruno on its payroll, and I question his motives. I know both of you work for Monsanto. Naturally, I wondered whether you knew that Bruno is paid by The De Reuterstad Group…Whether you knew *why*?" Standt was pleased he remembered the Dutch company's name.

"They pay Bruno the big bucks every month," he added, when Betsy didn't say anything right away.

"What's your evidence?" Betsy asked. "Are you insinuating something about Monsanto, and poor Amanda?"

"Poor Amanda," Standt repeated, bristling. He was

getting tightly wrapped inside this case and he took it personally. The patronizing attitudes were getting to him.

"Wouldn't you suspect something, given the same information?" he said. "Nobody here seems to care about Amanda, about really finding out what happened to her. The lead guy in the case has a cockamamie theory, and gets paid big bucks every month by Monsanto."

"I don't know anything about that..." she said. That seemed to ring true. Then Standt noticed Ted Rand and Bruno approaching them through the crowd at a rapid clip.

"So I want to know why this Group pays off Bruno, and why he's obfuscating–dragging his feet on–the Wilcox case." Standt said this directly to Ted Rand, who wore a cold, entitled smile.

Betsy also looked at her husband, but her expression was more curious and speculative, as if she was digesting this new angle.

Bruno came up alongside the detective and placed his ponderous mitt on Standt's shoulder. A tight grip.

"What are *you* doing here?" he said loudly, then seemed to blanch and apologized to the Rands.

"He was telling me about some monthly payments you receive from us–the company," Betsy said, but she aimed a faintly accusatory look at Ted Rand.

"Mr. Standt here doesn't seem to be in a party mood," Rand said.

"Look pal, you're going to have to leave. You can't come into the club like gangbusters and bother the patrons. This ain't New York, know what I mean? You gotta take your business elsewhere."

Standt brushed Bruno's hand off his shoulder like it was lint.

"How come you didn't tell me about the Monsanto employment? Isn't that a conflict of interest on Kauai?"

Bruno was turning blood red.

"The Sheriff does some routine security service for us. There's no conflict," Rand said, as though brushing aside a petty squabble. Then he reached into his pocket, pulled out a wad of bills, and peeled off four hundreds. He handed them to Standt.

"This will take care of your tickets. And more. Now move along. You can even stay at the party if you want, but stay out of my face. And stop prying into my employer's business, without warrant."

Standt ignored the bills.

"Who's the De Reuterstad Group?" Standt asked, firmly. "What do they have to do with Bruno Reilly...and Amanda?"

Ted Rand was now glaring at Bruno, and turning red himself. Everybody seemed to be a big drinker in this crowd, Standt thought. They wore the booze as a spreading red stain on their bodies. They all needed relaxation therapy.

Suddenly Bruno had seized Standt and was dragging him with both hands toward the entrance. After just a few feet of this, Reilly ended smashed over on his side, on the floor, and bellowing with pain.

After Standt had thrust the big awkward man to the floor and pulled Bruno's arm up behind his back, he put his lips close to the Sheriff's ear. He smelled stale cigarettes and rancid booze breath.

"Tell me what you know about the Wilcox case. What does Monsanto have to do with it? Tell me now!"

"Fuck you!"

They were surrounded by a small group of well-dressed people, all exuding shocked disapproval at Bruno's compromised position, and Standt's choke hold on him. As Bruno lay on the floor, his belly hung out of his untucked shirt and the tops of his buttocks showed in a slovenly manner behind some boxer shorts.

"Why are you fucking up the Wilcox case? What do you have to hide?"

"You're out of your frickin' mind, shit face. Get off me! She died on the ocean. Case closed." Bruno was out of breath and sweating profusely.

"Now let me up before we both get arrested."

They'd caused a huge commotion. Two big guys–a couple of Samoan football lineman that the club had hired–converged on them. Standt let go of Bruno's arm then let himself be gruffly escorted to the exit doors by the burly men.

He hadn't taken the $400 from Rand. He thought about the $250 tickets, when just outside the clubhouse he saw Katie walking quickly across the parking lot toward him.

"Just get lost pal," one of the bouncers said. "You're *persona non grata* at the club. We'll get you arrested the next time we see you around here. So scram."

Then Katie was by his side. "What the hell happened?"

"I was asking Ted Rand too many questions, I guess." Standt was faintly embarrassed. He was hoping this social fiasco wouldn't get back to Sam Wilcox.

"Come along," Katie said. "I have the car."

"I'll walk," Standt said. He wanted to air out his agitation. "I'll see you back at the condo. Know how to get there?"

"Yeah. You sure?"

"Yes."

Standt walked quickly with long strides down Ka Haku Road. The stars were bright, and there was a nice breeze. But he was frustrated. He didn't get enough time with the Rands. Betsy seemed interested, intrigued. She didn't know about the pay-offs. He thought he might have triggered something in her, but now he probably wouldn't be able to get close enough to the Rands again.

He fished around in his pocket for the cell phone as he walked. He wanted to call Chris K. He heard one of the off-kilter roosters crow in the darkness as he dialed the number.

CHAPTER 20: A TOUR BY HELICOPTER

"It took you what? Four days to have a scrap with Bruno?" Chris laughed loudly over the phone, pleasantly amused. "They're going to throw you off of Kauai."

"They should learn how to investigate murder cases here."

"Listen. You're not going to make any progress here throwing your weight around. This is Hawaii, not New York. People don't like violence, especially from out-of-towners. You're acting like a crazy haole. This the best way to get thrown off Kauai. That won't do Amanda any good. Even Bruno has gotten mellower."

"He's Ted Rand's pathetic pit bull. Doesn't seem mellow to me."

"I'm gonna have to give you some more Maui Wowie. Settle you down…"

"Bruno's totally on the take. He's a rotten cop."

"You're on the Rand's shit list now. You might give that a rest. I don't think they had anything to do with Amanda's disappearing."

Standt was walking back down Kamehameha Road, tucking his shirt back in. The breeze revived him.

"What do you think Bruno's up to then?"

"Making some extra bread, like everyone on Kauai. Monsanto has everyone on the payroll. They have endless moolah, right? Money talks, the old cliche. They're here to make money, and to do that you gotta spend some. On people. In the right places. Hey, I don't like it either. Seems sleazy. But I don't think Ted Rand got Amanda disappeared. An haole asshole, yeah. But a psychopath, no. These upper class guys don't act like that, it's not part of their…"

"Their M.O., right, I heard that before."

Standt watched Katie cruise past in the car, then pull up to the condo.

"Why don't you get some sleep…give the rough stuff a rest. The bad-ass stuff don't work in Hawaii, my friend."

"Seems like there're enough bad-asses here on the island to go around, to me."

Standt shifted gears away from the Rands.

"Ever heard of Doug Manley?"

Chris made a sound in the back of his throat like he'd swallowed something rancid.

"Sure I have. Arrested him once. Selling coke to the tourists in front of the Sheraton in Poipu."

"He's one of the bad asses you tell me don't exist on Kauai…"

"Yeah, okay. Agreed. He's bad."

"Amanda rented her board from the Manleys."

"So."

"Well, they never said anything after she disappeared.

Never reclaimed the board. Nobody ever looked into it. Don't you think that's strange?"

"They probably wanted nothing to do with it. Better let things slide. Brad Manley's a good guy. Probably thought the board had bad mojo."

Standt was suddenly beside himself. "Do people just go by vibes and mojo around here, or does anyone follow rational thoughts and reasoning? Did you check on the board and this…Samba Surf & Sport? They have a felon that works for them. Pretty violent guy. Maybe Amanda actually did return with the board onshore, but something really bad happened to her."

"Something bad happened to Amanda…I don't disagree with that. But let's take up this Manley stuff tomorrow. In fact, we're going to be flying over some of his territory."

"Territory? What is he, a different species?"

"In a manner of speaking he is a different kind of animal. You're going on the helicopter, right?"

"Is this just a tourist flight?"

"No. Think of it as search and rescue. For Amanda."

That shifted his thinking and emotions somewhat. His heart beat heavily with the memory of mashing Bruno's jowly face into the clubhouse linoleum. He thought of maybe pouring a tall white wine and standing on the bluff and the grass and staring at the ocean to calm down. At least he was beginning to learn the Hawaiian medicine for what ails people.

"Okay. I'll be there."

# # #

It was 10 a.m. the next day. Standt and Katie drove down to Lihue and met Chris Ke' alohilani on the tarmac alongside the airport helipad. An A-STAR helicopter awaited them, its loud, metallic rotor blades slicing the air about once per second.

The aircraft reminded Standt of the news choppers he saw in the skies of Manhattan. Except this one was painted with a fancy tropical scene–the lime-green leaves of a palm tree with the sun setting behind it on distant mountains.

The helicopter seemed poised to lift off the helipad and fly away at any moment. Then the passenger door swung open and a man in a wide-brimmed safari hat stepped down, smiled, and beckoned for the three passengers to board.

Chris let Standt sit upfront with the pilot; he and Katie sat in back. The pilot was a friend of Chris', a former Marine helicopter captain from Oklahoma City named Abner Vereen.

He had a southwestern twang and a hail-fellow-well-met manner. As Katie boarded, he gave her a gentleman's tip of the hat.

Whatever military experience he'd had, Vereen had landed a peach of a job now in his retirement from the service; ferrying tourists in and out of Kauai's spectacular topography. They aimed for dramatic locations Hollywood had once used for movies, like *South Pacific* or *Jurassic Park*.

Abner had a brownish red beard, an unruly shock of gray-streaked hair stuffed into the bush hat, and a raffish smile that revealed several missing molars.

He turned around and looked at the two passengers in the backseat, then grinned ear to ear at Standt. The acrophobic detective gripped the edge of his seat and tried to make it seem that Vereen and his powerful aircraft didn't terrify him.

"Ready?"

"About as ready as I ever will be."

Standt thought of the helicopter crash in the Hudson during the 1990s; how it had changed his life. After he'd rescued the boy in the freezing Hudson he'd met his glamorous wife Lara. They'd fought on a more or less continuous basis, but at least they'd produced Tim amidst the skirmishes.

That reminded him he had to talk to Tim soon; the lad lived in a nice townhouse in Manhattan with his mother.

"Off we go folks!"

The chopper lifted off the helipad as though it was light as a feather, then it tilted to the side and accelerated, quickly gaining altitude over a nearby stand of trees. The flat-roofed airport buildings got smaller as they ascended.

Then the aircraft arched over the Pacific Ocean. Standt wore the protection over his ears, he could see the ubiquitous tiny wavelets that flecked the dark blue seas off Kauai, and made it difficult to distinguish the boats from the endless wind-driven sea. Then the chopper leaned left and headed north to the Napali Coast.

Chris gestured down to Hanalei Bay, and Standt got a quick view of the north shore coastline and the bluff where they were staying at Princeville.

"It's Amanda's route on the paddleboard," Chris yelled out over the engine. "We'll double back over it later."

Vereen gave Standt a quick, intrigued look, as in "What's this guy's schtick here?"

Chris must have filled in his pilot friend already, about the New York detective looking for the famous missing lady.

Then the helicopter swung over the impossibly steep and sharply ridged coastline of Napali, choked with dark green vegetation that made it look like Borneo or Papua New Guinea.

Katie snapped pictures out the window as they flew about four thousand feet over Napali's beautiful white crescent-shaped beaches, with azure water slapping against a surrounding reef.

Chris looked out the window, smiling, and pointing things out to Katie. Standt had smelled weed on him that morning. It was amusing that a police investigator in Hawaii was so blase about his own pot smoking. Standt wondered whether the surfer was high–it would make sense that he might want to be buzzed for the vistas proffered by the helicopter ride.

But the detective hoped to God that *Vereen* hadn't toked up with the surfer, for all of their safety's sake. At any rate, he couldn't smell any pot on Abner, and Chris' aroma could have just been derived from the night before and still clung to his clothes.

The helicopter dipped into a canyon that bisected the Napali Coast.

"We're heading into Waimea Canyon," Vereen yelled over. "It's a couple thousand feet on either side."

They were surrounded by steep, red rocky slopes that looked like a strip-mining operation. They were heavily eroded. A dry river bed lay below, then yellowed trees and shrubs grew up the slopes on either side.

"What goes on in here?" Standt said.

"Hunting, and hiking."

"What do they hunt?"

"Wild pigs, some deer."

Off to the left, out the window, the tangled wet slopes above the canyon, with ridges jutting through them like spinal cords, rose to a mountain engulfed in dark gray clouds.

"Anyone ever go up to that mountain?" Standt yelled to Vereen.

"Only scientists, mostly, studying the flora and fauna. And only by helicopter. They want more hunters because the pigs trample the rare plants. But it's too difficult to walk into this terrain."

The helicopter had traversed a large swath of Waimea Canyon in just the few minutes of their conversation. Vereen, still wearing his trademark safari hat, pulled back on the controls, executing a climb up one of the slopes. Then the helicopter swung around to exit the canyon.

Vereen looked at Standt then back to the controls.

"So I heard you're looking for that Amanda lady."

"Right."

"A shame, a real shame. Heard she was a nice young girl."

"What else did you hear?" Standt said. He figured Abner was about as attune to the island's gossip and goings on as Chris, maybe more so because of the diversity of his clientele.

Vereen shook his head. "Nothing, really. Knew she led the movement against GMO. I'm all for that. Get the experiments off the island."

"Do you hear a lot about that here?"

"Yes. Sometimes I take the Monsanto folks for tours. In fact, they're some of my best customers."

"Did they ever mention Amanda Wilcox?"

"No. Who you work for?"

"Her father."

Vereen shook his head again, straightened his shoulders.

"I feel bad for him. They'll never find her…I mean…" He was reluctant to sound defeatist.

"I wish you the best of luck. I hope you find out something. But when you disappear in the ocean around here, and you don't get found right away, the chances are slim."

"Where are we going right now?"

"We're going back to the north shore and over the interior of the island. I want to show you the forest. The boonies."

"Where do you live?" Standt asked.

"Wailua. I love it. Nice little town." He yelled over the engine noise, and the high velocity wind outside. "Got me a bungalow with my lady. Pretty beach nearby."

"Got any kids?"

"No. You?"

"Yeah. A son, Tim. Back in New York."

"Nice. I like kids. But I think my time has come and gone. I'm too old now to get the kid thing started."

"Where'd you serve?"

Abner looked at him and the toothy grin that accompanied most of his comments vanished from his face.

"Desert Storm. Yeah '91, flew a Blackhawk helicopter for Air Cav." Then he began looking back over the terrain beneath them, as though quietly comparing it to the Middle Eastern desert.

"The desert is tough. Hard on the engines. Sucks up the sand."

"How long you been doing this?"

There were no signs of any people, or evidence anyone had ever hiked along beneath them, just rocks, the ubiquitous red earth of Kauai, and sparse trees and island vegetation that belied the tangled jungles that choked the steep terrain above the canyon.

"Twenty years, since after Hurricane Aniki in '92."

"Wow."

Then they emerged from the canyon, bursting out upon a dramatic oceanic view. They flew out over the Napali Coast and Kalalau Beach.

Standt could see a large beautiful yacht moored off the shore. It seemed the perfect portrait of exclusive isolation. Vereen could see him gazing at it.

"Not a bad scene huh?"

The helicopter shot up the coast north, alongside the sheer cliffs of the island. The steep rock walls sprouted waterfalls and dripped with vast blankets of mossy green vegetation.

Katie leaned forward from the backseat, with a digital camera dangling from a strap around her neck.

"Can I come here and live? On that yacht?"

Chris had been pointing things out to her. Standt wondered when the Amanda part of the trip was going to take place. Their scouting of her route.

Within a few minutes they were back up over Hanalei Bay. It seemed empty from that height; you could hardly make out the swimmers and surfers. It was pale blue with regions of different colors, shades of blue, purple, and aquamarine. A small swell broke over the reef offshore.

Then Chris leaned forward, taking Katie's place.

"We can see her whole route. She started over there at the St. Regis." He pointed toward the bulky hotel thrusting out from the shoreline. Abner put the helicopter into a descent and made a comment about using the rotor wash to knock off bikini tops. "I call it the 'tit tour'," he laughed, and Standt couldn't help but laugh his head off with him.

"What did he say?" Katie said from the backseat, and Standt just looked back at her and smiled.

The people wandering the beach and spread out on the chaise lounges shielded their eyes and looked up at the passing chopper.

"Another pass like that and the St. Regis lawyers will kill us," Abner quipped.

"She usually went down the river there." As they swung out over the point that jutted into the sea just south of the hotel and its beach, Standt looked back to the river. It looked very narrow from that height. It was a different color than the sea, a more murky green.

From that height, it looked like a painter had passed a different colored brush over it.

"Where does it go?"

"Not far, becomes very narrow. People on paddleboards turn around and go back out into Hanalei Bay."

The helicopter reconnoitered around the point where the paddleboard washed up. That spot was a long way from the river. Standt caught Chris looking at him.

"The board should have washed up on the beach alongside the bay," the surfer said.

Vereen navigated the helicopter away from the coast again and headed west, into the mountains. The knobby terrain was cloaked in dark, gray clouds that seemed about to burst. The summits' shrouds had a dank, permanent quality to them.

"Where are we going?" Standt asked the pilot.

"Past the demilitarized zone, into boonie land. Where only helicopters fear to tread."

Chris leaned forward.

"There's another part of Amanda's territory I wanted to show you first," he said.

He pointed down to some farmland, first a large cornfield and then other crops, which looked like coffee then pineapples or papaya. Vereen brought them down several hundred feet and they flew over acres and acres of crops.

Sometimes they were low enough that the leaves of the trees and the plants bent back against the wake of the rotor blades.

"Those are GMO plantings, by farmers paid by Monsanto."

"How do you know?"

"It's common knowledge. Amanda led some protests in there. They drove and hiked in with signs and loudspeakers. It was a big deal. It drew a lot of media attention to this area."

"When?"

Chris's black stringy mustache drooped down over his lips. Standt, faintly, could still smell the weed. Katie was listening, taking some notes, looking out the window.

"Just a few months ago." Then he looked at Vereen and said, "Go into Cambodia."

Vereen pointed the helicopter along the green tangled laps of the slopes that led up to the cloud-cloaked summits. The sun shined through spaces in the clouds and illuminated light-green ponds of overgrowth. Then the helicopter zoomed along the slopes. It was tiny next to the mountainside.

"We call it Cambodia. It's a kind of no man's land. No one lives up here. Few can ever come here. It's all mud and muck and insects and rain. But we think there's a lot of narcotics grown back here. We *know* it."

"How?"

"Word gets around. Like the guy who had the fight with Doug Manley. Said Manley had a major crop back here. There's a lot of money to be made in growing poppies, cocaine, hashish, and many many points to take it off the island in boats to the big markets on the mainland. Then on to Los Angeles…

"Trouble is, Cambodia is not that far from the GMO plantations. It's Monsanto's land. They don't want anyone snooping around here."

Standt craned his neck and looked down at the terrain they flew over: just green, dense jungle; no roads, paths, or rows of plants.

"What about the DEA? The feds?"

"Not interested."

"Why?"

"Don't know. Monsanto? Maybe they lobbied the

federal government to lay off these slopes–too close for comfort. To close to Monsanto's GMO experiments."

"Cambodia…" Abner repeated in a low whisper, then turned the chopper around to make another pass. The ride was making Standt sick, and in the last few minutes he'd sensed a cold sweat building.

He mumbled to Chris: "Ever intercept any of this contraband crop?"

"Never. Not yet. Anyways, you mentioned that Amanda rented her board from Manley. Maybe Doug was her guy behind the counter. Her protests were the closest any Kauai people typically would get to Manley's crop, to Cambodia.

"Maybe they, she, stumbled on to something. In fact, it wouldn't be too hard for anyone who spends a lot of time back there to maybe…come across some hidden poppies, masquerading as something else. Papayas. Maybe Manley has an investor and they can spend a lot of money on camouflage."

Vereen was smiling through his shaggy beard, pleased at having someone with which to share their Cambodia secret.

"Why didn't you tell me this before?" Standt said.

Chris thought for a moment. "Let's just say I had a kind of revelation, when you told me about Amanda and Doug Manley."

"So how does this story play out in your mind?" Standt wiped the cold sweat off his brow. The helicopter had air conditioning that did not mesh well with the humidity outside. It was like being trapped in the trunk of a car and having cold air blowing on your head. "Manley did something to Amanda? We question Manley."

"It'd be worth it. But we have to go through his lawyer. He's in trouble right now. But it makes sense to me.

Get records of the rental. Find out where Manley was when Amanda disappeared. What do you think Ab?"

Vereen looked behind him. "We go back to Lihue."

Standt sat back in his seat, swallowed back the faint nausea, and quietly watched the terrain flatten and spread out to grassy meadows, roads, and bungalows; plantations and dirt paths. Kauai was more densely populated along the coast as they approached Lihue and prepared to set the chopper down.

By the time they'd landed, Standt had reached his limits for the high-altitude exploration of the Garden Isle. He bent down and disembarked from the helicopter then ran across the tarmac to a clump of trees, scattering a few wild chickens, and puked.

The others leapt down from the aircraft, stood off to the side, and watched Standt's sojourn to the edges of the runway. Then he slowly walked back to the group, wiping his mouth with a handkerchief. When he rejoined them, Katie put her arm around his shoulder, and they all walked over to the terminal.

CHAPTER 21: TRACING DATA

Standt spent part of that afternoon tracking down the elusive Manleys. He wanted an interview with both of them.

The package from Sam Wilcox containing the records of Amanda's phone calls and credit card records lay on a table. He knifed open the envelope and began plowing through them. He was still feeling the addled, acrophobic effects of the helicopter ride, so he wasn't eating anything at the moment.

Katie sat on a chair outside facing the ocean, typing on her laptop. They were going to eat in that night, dining on seafood that Katie had fetched from The Dolphin Center. Wilcox's condo had a nice kitchen.

# # #

Amanda's phone and credit-card records were a treasure trove. Despite his trust of Standt and his motivation to find Amanda, it was still odd that Wilcox had tore open the guts of her private life for the detective. The data could have been lifted directly from the records of the National Security Agency (NSA).

He had a whole two months of it, but he only decided to pay attention to the last three weeks. The eight days she was missing were, of course, empty. No credit card purchases, no telephone calls. So no one who had taken her and her belongings was using her credit card. No pleas or cries for help. The NSA can only go so far. One can still disappear off the radar screen in America.

Twelve days ago she'd had dinner at a South Shore restaurant called Brennike's. The outing had to have been with several people, because her credit card was charged $160. How could a non-profit campaigner afford that? She must have had a bankroll from Sam Wilcox.

Amanda had another purchase the same day from Nukumoi Surf Shop, a non-chafing sport shirt, probably a gift for her own paddleboarding. So she was with people, and doing something on the posh south shore of the island that day.

There were a couple of telephone calls to Manhattan, perhaps to her father and/or Dash Crenshaw, unless he'd slipped out of her romantic picture by then. All Standt had were cell-phone numbers, but they were easily decoded.

Standt was surprised, and pleased to find in the bottom of the stack of personal records, an archive of her emails and Web-page requests. The information was so dense and voluminous and revealing, that he felt guilty delving into it. It would be particularly crass and ghoulish if she was dead. He felt like he was sifting through her linen drawer.

But he needed this level of detail for his investigation.

He fell asleep with the stack of papers on his chest.

He dreamt he was caught offshore treading water in a never-ending succession of waves. He bobbed up and down, barely able to keep his head above the frothy seas. He was being swept out to the horizon.

Each new wave hovered above him like a black menace, then he rode the trough of the swell up to the crest and flailed his legs and arms to keep from being pitched over the top and hurtled to the bottom.

Just above the surface of the agitated sea, in the distance, he saw a long-haired woman clinging to a paddleboard. Her hair was wet, matted, and clung to her upper back. She faced away from him; he couldn't see her face. She had on a wetsuit revealing the long sinewy arms as she kept trying to throw a leg over the board and get back on.

"Amanda!" he cried, gasping for air, treading water, keeping the sea out of his mouth. "Amanda!" She ignored him.

When she finally turned her head to him, a woman across the water, he thought he recognized Amanda but he couldn't be sure. She began to say something to him but it was just mouthing words. He tried to make out what she was saying, because he had the dream sensation that the words had great meaning. It was essential that he understand them.

She kept repeating the same mouthed phrase, but he couldn't decipher it. Each new wave drove him farther away.

He heard loud music in the same room where he was sleeping. He opened his eyes and got up sluggishly. He was still submerged in the seas of his dream; it was if the water was dripping off him. He walked over to the door of his bedroom.

He saw the outlines of a large person in his living room, framed by the moonlight. An odd ethereal light. The loud pop music was coming from just outside the sliding glass door. It was a wild party, but it still seemed like he was dreaming.

What was this form doing in his living room? Now

there were two hulking presences. He moved forward to the living room, barefoot, no shirt, a pair of boxer shorts on. The two men floated forward through the half darkness to meet him.

Standt felt around for the revolver that wasn't there, and by the time he thought of seizing another weapon, the two men had him by each arm. They dragged him to the sliding glass door.

He wasn't sleeping anymore. "What the fuck?" he cried out, recognizing the stale odor of an overwrought, unwashed male given off by Bruno Reilly.

"You're not listening to reason these days," Bruno grumbled. "So we're going to teach you some."

The other man on his left arm had to have weighed about 280 or 300 pounds. Standt looked up into his large round face and recognized one of the Samoans from the golf club.

Bruno struggled with the sliding glass door. For a moment, Standt broke free, but once he did he felt a blunt, hard chop to his left shoulder by the Samoan. It felt more like a body blow. That dropped him to his knees, which was the posture he was in when they pulled him across the grass lawn beneath the palm trees, and out to the edge of the bluff.

The calm surf broke off the reef and rolled into large black rocks about one hundred feet in the darkness below.

# # #

"Do you know what you did to me back at the golf club?" Bruno screamed over the wind.

It whipped the palm fronds back and forth against a star-studded sky. He was enraged.

"You lost me my job, that's what! The Monsanto guys dropped me like a hot potato! I need that money. I have alimony. Lawyers! Five grand a month!"

"You *have* a job!" Standt struggled again with his pinioned arms. "Let go, assholes! What are you trying to prove?"

He could sense blood trickling out of the edge of his left nostril onto his upper lip. It seemed the Samoan had clipped him there, too. Everything on his left side seemed tender; he felt the glow and spread of a shoulder bruise. At least, his nose wasn't broken.

He wouldn't want to have anything permanent in life that would force him to remember Bruno.

"You're a sheriff on Kauai. Remember?"

"That doesn't pay shit! My pension's drying up back in Boston. I needed that gig! After that crap you pulled at Princeville Golf, Rand told me to take a shiner! *Poor performance*, he said. 'You're makin' people think Monsanto had something to do with Amanda Wilcox.'"

"He said that?"

"People won't leave it alone, he said."

"This doesn't sound like my fault…"

They pushed him closer to the edge, so that his left leg dangled pathetically over the dry shrubs that edged the cliff. The moonlight glittered on the lapping waters in the distance below.

"I got one more opportunity, and that's to get you off the island. He might reconsider. So tell Wilcox you're done for the week. You're leaving tomorrow morning. Get the New York fat cat to buy you a flight home. Or you get pitched onto the rocks. Believe me, it's happened before. A tourist gets drunk and walks off the bluff in their sleep. You were acting pretty drunk the other night."

"That's insane. I'm not leaving tomorrow."

Standt felt like an idiot, like some drunk who was being eighty-sixed from a bar. He only had boxer shorts on, and a roll of fat had worked its way over his waist from many

Manhattan dinners out with Katie and the last several days in Hawaii.

He was slipping, in his fifties. He was inching toward becoming the pitiable knucklehead he usually judged harshly.

"Tell me you're outa here, or you're gonna be more shark feed on the reef," Bruno grumbled. Standt wondered if the washed-up cop had learned these shenanigans in Boston, in Whitey Bulger's territory.

Standt didn't say anything but struggled vainly against the combined weight of the Samoan and Bruno, maybe 500 pounds pressing him over the bluff, then:

"Let him go! Now! I said now!"

It was Katie. She had a huge, broad kitchen knife pointed, like a sword, at the back of the Samoan's head, where the spinal cord connects to the skull.

"Ever heard of Kendo?" she whispered. She'd gotten some martial arts training in Manhattan, with swords. Mostly for discipline and fitness, but she'd done it since she was a teenager.

But there was nothing mystical about the knife she pointed with both hands at Standt's assailant. It had a long, serrated blade. She'd stepped back just out of range of a kick by him, but one thrust from her could do some nasty damage.

The Samoan turned a half head, with a sheepish look. He seemed half hearted about this assault on Standt. "Yeah…I heard of Kendo."

As those two were having their little conversation, Standt brought his club-like right foot down hard on to the soft top of Bruno's foot. Bruno bellowed with pain, as Standt wrestled free. Katie stood back about another foot, still aiming the kitchen knife at the Samoan's ample flesh.

With all three of them poised on the edge of the precipice, in a kind of indecisive tableau, Standt used the opportunity to plant his fist firmly into Bruno's abdomen, sending him down to the grass in a groaning heap.

Then he scrambled back to the safety of the grassy lawn. He was really beginning to wonder about the local law enforcement, with Bruno being the one in charge.

Now all they could do was shoot him, but with Katie present, that option was greatly compromised. And Bruno still lay groaning and writhing on the ground. The Samoan dropped his arms. He stood in the darkness, shaking his head, with a "What the fuck am I doing here?" vibe.

He was a huge guy, but Standt didn't have the impression he ever would have thrown the detective onto the rocks. Too much risk, very little advantage to him. Another dead haole was not worth the trouble to him. What were they, paying him by the hour?

As they remained there silently, Bruno got to his knees and stood up unsteadily. He had an untucked Hawaiian shirt pulled over a paunch, and hairy, slightly bowed legs.

"This ain't over…"

"I can dial 911 right now," Katie said, getting out her cell phone. "And have you both arrested for assault with an intent to murder."

Standt looked at her proudly and said softly, feeling over the left side of his body, "Don't bother. I'd say we're about even."

The Samoan looked at Bruno. "Let's get out of here."

He didn't seem a bad type. He'd just gotten involved with the wrong crowd. Standt wondered if he was on Monsanto's payroll, too.

The detective put a towel he found on a chair around his shoulders. Then he aimed a question at the Samoan: "What do *you* think happened to Amanda Wilcox?"

The Samoan looked to the ocean stretching for thousands of miles to the horizon and beyond, as if searching for timeworn knowledge from his elders.

"She's out there, a long ways," he said with a kind of gruff wisdom. "She's gone off Kauai."

As if on cue, they all turned away. Standt stood on the lawn until the Samoan and Reilly had started up their car and driven away toward Kamehameha Road. Then Standt and Katie opened the sliding glass door, went into the condo, and locked it behind them.

CHAPTER 22: THE BUSH

Standt couldn't sleep. He put some ice on his shoulder and made some tea. Katie still wanted to call the police. But who *was* the police?

Where was the law and order on the north shore? It was hard to trust anyone on the island now, with Bruno's rottenness glaringly on display.

If it wasn't for Katie…things hadn't gone so honky dory for Standt since he'd arrived in Kauai. He still had flimsy leads.

He was leaning in Chris' direction. Bruno was just a bad cop open to pay-offs from all comers. Standt wasn't convinced that Reilly had anything to do with the vanishing of Amanda.

Standt began to sift through Amanda's credit-card records. One pattern jumped out. Amanda made three appearances at the St. Regis, all within a week and a half. And obviously, she paid the bills. Who was she with? Why'd she go to that expensive bar so much? It must have been a regular meeting. He would call the waitress, Carla. She was in the know. She seemed to be holding something back.

He looked at the phone records for the week. Several calls came in to Amanda's cell phone from the same number, multiple times per day, often unanswered. They were local calls, a Kauai number. He would have it traced. Wilcox would do that for him.

Standt stood up and departed to the bathroom to splash some water on his face. Katie, his lover ninja, had passed out. He looked at his face in the mirror, unshaven and bruised from recent skirmishes.

Kauai, its odd, unsettling equatorial influence on people, making them grasp for extremes and ever more largesse than they deserved or worked for, had had him back pedaling. He needed to resolve the case. Then he wasn't sure whether he'd ever come back to Kauai. Maybe the Big Island or Maui under different circumstances.

He dabbed more water on his face, which radiated bruising and defeat and sleeplessness.

He returned to the phone records. Amanda had made a few calls out to Manhattan. Probably to her father, maybe to Dash Crenshaw. He didn't see anything else in the cell phone list, only the repeated calls to her phone at around the same time she was making multiple visits at sundown to the St. Regis terrace.

He moved on to the records of her Web-page visits. Katie was still passed out. He knew he should get some sleep, not keep going all the way to sun-up. There was the Doug Manley lead to pursue.

# # #

Doug Manley gunned the old Ford 450 up the red dusty road through the weeds. The road hadn't been repaired in years. The tires seemed to go airborne and land with a sickening series of thuds. He didn't want to break a strut or an axle. Well, that would cause him to go ballistic all over again, given the mood he was in.

Doug had dirty blond hair that hung lankly past his shoulders. Small black crucifixes were embedded in his earlobes. He stroked a chin covered with a scraggly three-week-old red beard. He looked at his eyes in the rear-view mirror, against a cloud of red dust the truck had kicked up. They were an angry raw red, since he'd been up since three in the morning.

He'd closed a couple of bars at one a.m., then took a bottle of rum alone to a lonely corner of Koa Kea Beach. He was there until three, brooding and commiserating with himself.

That's where he slept, his truck tucked away in the bushes. Wandering back up the beach at some unknown hour in the morning, he'd run into a couple of middle-aged, wishy-washy hippies who were still trying to live off of papayas, coconuts, and Maui Wowie. Then a couple of meth heads staggered past him.

Even *he* seemed sober compared with them.

After a 16-ounce to-go coffee bought in Hanalei Town, he finally called his lawyer back. The news wasn't good. He was due to appear in front of a judge in Lihue. They were setting the date soon. He wanted to plead not guilty to assault, but this hairball was going to tie him up in knots indefinitely.

That's when he'd bought a bottle of mescal tequila and drove his truck out of town until the roads turned dark red with a dust that the rain could never keep down.

He was driving into Cambodia, and maybe he wouldn't look back. There were huts he could stay in, food and water. Plenty of weed. His brother Brad wasn't going to be any help. He'd previously threatened to refuse any bail if Doug got in trouble again, did some thing that was beyond the shadow of a doubt his fault.

Doug broke things, like the law, ever since they were kids, and Brad had finally run out of patience, trying to fix them. Not even surfing could cure Doug.

He reached over and seized the tequila bottle and thrust it to his lips. He sucked greedily on the top of the bottle and bubbles broke along the inside of the glass, then he set it back on the seat with a rough vengeance.

The drink was harsh and smooth at the same time. He was tripping on it. The tequila made his thoughts jump around and then return to justifications that explained why people always tried to hate and persecute him, blame him, cheat him out of the good deal.

Given the circumstances of his date in court, Doug had to accelerate their original plan. Which was to package up the hashish, heroin, and coke that they'd already harvested and use their two motor boats to move it to the Big Island ASAP.

He had a couple of guys and a gal who worked for him. Despite the way they looked, they weren't weird to him. They did their jobs.

He looked around him, the truck engulfed in red dust, tires bumping off of ruts and exposed roots. Long jacaranda and bamboo branches stroked the fenders and doors as he roughly maneuvered the vehicle. Going into Cambodia made him feel under control again. The jungle exuded a certain foggy power.

The road narrowed to a point where it didn't look navigable anymore, but he knew the route. He was getting close to the hut, the crude but serviceable one. No one can find him out here, not even the law. Not even Brad. His brother called it "the bush." He didn't know about the

"Cambodia" name.

Anywhere Brad didn't bother to go on Kauai in the mountains he called "the bush." He knew that's where Doug went, when Doug was being bad. He could tell the authorities that Doug was probably in the backcountry, but he couldn't pinpoint exactly where. Then the helicopters would have to be brought in, but so far, they'd always left him alone.

The crop was heavy, thriving. He could get very rich on this cargo, maybe retire off Kauai, where he was notorious, to a luxury condo in Maui. He could get rich without the Columbians, the Mexicans. They were nutcases anyways; totally psycho. But this guy he'd pulled a knife on, that was a problem, the lawyers and district attorney wouldn't let it go.

There was another bit of business that was still a thorn in his side. Not bad enough to make him stay on Kauai indefinitely, but it *was* an issue. A crumpled up newspaper sat on the seat beside him. He'd used it to wrap the tequila bottle in on his way out the door and through the parking lot of the liquor store.

He picked it up, just as the truck pulled up to the hut. He slammed on the brakes and churned up another red dust cloud.

Laney was outside hanging wet laundry, and she waved quickly at him, grinning her nearly toothless smile. Doug smiled himself; the hut seemed like home. He was safe. It was really out there, the clouded mountaintop looming above them. They often sat in the hut and drank tequila or rum and smoked hash and watched the rain come down.

Laney had sold bootleg Vicodin in Lihue. That's how he had first met her. They'd hit it off pretty quickly. She was a whacko chick but she knew her business.

For the both of them, the money was in drugs, not low-level behind-the-counter work at stores or surf shops.

The mood that came over them in the rain out there in Cambodia seemed like a kind of shared wisdom.

He opened up the crumpled newspaper to the pretty lady's face. The headline said "Police Seek More Clues In Amanda Wilcox Case."

The glamorous girl smiled out of the newspaper, as if she knew and loved anyone who would be reading it.

The people of Kauai were beginning to forget about her, tired of never being able to escape the continuous refrain of "Where's Amanda?" All the media types on the island, somewhat like locusts even to the islanders who were used to their home being photographed and idealized.

Those people were beginning to leave, to disperse. Amanda was like a winner of *American Idol* that people couldn't remember the name of anymore.

He picked the bottle up and shook it; a pickled worm moved about in an inch and a half of tequila. He dropped the newspaper to the floor of the cab, Amanda's now crinkled face looking up at him in the humid, mote-filled air.

He guzzled down the bottle, including the worm, before he shut the truck door and hurled the bottle into the moist jungle that all but engulfed the hut.

CHAPTER 23: ECSTASY

Church was stretched out on his long narrow mattress in the Brooklyn apartment, large hands folded behind his head. His eyes were open, and he still had a black leather coat on and the pointed, dorky-brown size-thirteen leather shoes that he seldom strayed from. His feet hung off the end of the bed.

A cheerless light from the street cast a warped rectangle on to his bare wall, which was in need of paint. Below that was his black computer set-up: a big flat-screen monitor next to a tower of multi-terabyte hard disks and powerful CPUs.

It was hot outside and the window was open. The humming of the CPUs mingled with the incessant street noise. It never really let up except for a few hours after three a.m. The buzz of activity was sporadically punctuated by the piercing screech of sirens.

He'd learned to sleep through them. You have to in

Brooklyn.

He hadn't heard from Standt in days, which was unusual. Standt said he had phone, cell, and Web records already for Amanda Wilcox. Maybe Standt didn't need Church. Maybe he was still pissed off about Church getting high.

Amanda was still in the newspapers but now they were printing rumors. Church wondered if Standt was in the thick of digging up the rumors, stuff about alternative theories. How she wasn't really killed by a shark. Church was oddly comforted by that notion (even though she was still probably dead); he hated the ocean and he hated sharks.

He figured Standt had to be at the center of shooting holes in the original theories.

iz was coming uptown. They were getting high again, and heading into Manhattan. Midtown. It seemed easier when Standt was out of town, his detective's influence and the policing of Church's behavior were absent for the moment. Maybe that wasn't such a good thing. Church needed this gig with Standt.

He and iz were getting high on a potent mixture then hanging out at a Midtown place called Dos Caminos. He bent his tall skinny frame off the bed, and stuffed his wallet in the back pocket of the heavily patched jeans. It was the place near his behind where the evidence of a buttocks would normally be apparent on a less emaciated person.

Then he took the rickety elevator down to the street and caught the next F Train into Manhattan.

The train was as hot as Mumbai. It was full of simmering and dissipated characters. The goddamn climate was changing and turning New York into an anvil of heat. One of those Third World countries where people are jammed close together by the millions and can never cool down.

He texted iz. The phrasing went like "on the F" then she answered ":)" and "in midtown soon" then another message beneath that: "chillin." He typed in with a flourish that took seconds: "30 min 50th + 3rd."

They were going to eat outside and just let the Midtown action flow over them. They had some bread to spend on good food and a great buzz. He kept motivated in the smelly subway by imagining the vision of a slinky iz standing on the corner waiting for him. Just him. Church. *His* girl. He never thought. It would happen. To him. To be this lucky.

iz was putting together the mixture. She was better at it than he was. It would be Ecstasy and a little downer, to take the crazy edge off.

He found her just where he thought he would, at 50th Street and Third Avenue, standing across the street from Dos Caminos. They kissed–how domestic feeling for Church, who normally hadn't kissed girls, *ever*–then they used a bottle of Pellegrino to wash down the pill mix, before heading across the street.

Dos Caminos had a big outdoors section, which was already crowded with people who wanted to dig the warm air and the sun going down while they drank their tequila and wine and listened to the pop music.

They were seated right beneath two speakers, and the friendly waiter noted, after giving their grunge clothes a silent once-over, that this was known as "the party table." Because it was so close to the speakers.

Both iz and Church nodded respectfully, then once the waiter turned and sped away, they burst out laughing. If only he knew…they ordered glasses of cold white wine and nachos.

The food was promptly ignored as Church could feel the warm elixir of narcotic buzz bloom like a flower growing inside him. iz looked hot, in a starlet way, some beautiful space maiden in a sci-fi film.

He liked her platinum blond hair and all the black leather and the way her hair was spiky and her rouge deep ruby red. It fit the evening-in-Manhattan vibe so well, with its loud pulsating, never-ending background music. Life as music video.

They ordered a virtual debauch of food, but ultimately only to admire it; the vivid colors of green (avocado), red (peppers), yellow (nacho chips and cheese), and assorted chili browns. They both faced the street and watched the world go by while a ten-minute mash-up composed of multiple influences went on and on through the speakers…Justin Timberlake followed by old Michael Jackson then Bob Marley and out of nowhere Frank Sinatra then back to Marley–it was just crazy, yet perfect and surprising, the way the song was pieced together with so many diverse influences but it never ended and boogied on and on and blended together with such perfection.

They looked at each other and smiled. iz was slightly nodding to the music, spot on the beat. He never wanted this night at Dos Caminos to end.

Out of nowhere a motorcade sped by–black SUVs and Lincoln Town Cars and NYPD squad cars and motorcycles, with sirens and lights going. Heading to some place like the United Nations, and speeding not ten yards from where they sat on 50th and Third. What a trip, it seemed to be arranged just for them.

He reached into his back pocket and removed a printed Kauai map that he'd scraped off the Web. He couldn't stop thinking about Kauai, about how Standt hadn't contacted him in what seemed like weeks (when you're high). About how he didn't know enough yet about the circumstances of Amanda Wilcox.

He felt hamstrung, not being in Kauai, or in front of the computer terminal right now. He stared at the map and seemed to smell the beach, feel its placid breezes. He was channeling Amanda, he finally decided, his big feet in the warm waters and the sun caressing the pallid face that saw so little sunlight.

As he stared at the green island on the map, the loud cover through the speakers settled on Bob Marley. *No woman no cry*… How fitting.

He studied the mountains in the center of the island. It was a black green blob and there seemed to be nothing there but mountains and jungle. He saw primeval humans hiding in there. He had to see this place: Kauai, the five thousand foot mountains and the jungles and the prettiest and most forbidding cliffs in the world, all of which had swallowed Amanda.

It was virtually Jurassic. The map was divided into micro-climate regions from dark green in the center to pale yellow on the coast. She'd left the coast, last seen there on her paddleboard, but somehow he couldn't take his eyes off the dark-green core of Kauai. It was the center of all meaning and mystery, where King Kong lived. No doubt. It was Kong Land.

He looked at iz, then back at the map. The music throbbed its scratchy Jamaican reggae rhythm. iz nodded, smiled prettily, at the sky, her eyes and jewelry all glittery. Then the music transitioned to Justin Timberlake, all of a sudden but once again, fitting and perfect, and iz glanced back at him giggling with Ecstasy pleasure. The whole tableau of her head, with its dangling silver ornaments, flashing eyes, and shoulder-length platinum hair, glowed with vivid vitality in the way of an Andy Warhol poster.

Warhol also painted Amanda in Church's head, a determined, unsmiling face framed by long blond hair and backlit by a brilliant sunrise. The vision suggested anything but a water-logged corpse. Her face was the picture of *life,* not death.

It was as though she'd already been deified by the Hawaiian worshipers. He thought that maybe rather than dead she was…he placed his finger on the Hanalei River and followed it up to its source, until the etched line vanished at the edges of the jungle.

CHAPTER 24: SURFING

"Vicodin addiction."

"Vicodin addiction treatment."

"Vicodin addiction treatment options."

These phrases kept appearing in the records of Amanda's Web searches. They showed up in the weeks before she disappeared. Standt wondered why she was she was so interested in Vicodin, an opiate painkiller used by millions.

The FDA wanted to cancel it years ago. So many overdoses. No way, said the manufacturer. We make too much money from it. So they use lobbyists to pressure the FDA. Vicodin still rules.

Did Amanda have a friend who got hooked on Vicodin? She seemed to be in great shape herself. It wasn't a subject that someone would idly search on. It raised a red flag. Was *she* hooked on it?

He was going to take the subject of Vicodin up with

Sam. If not Wilcox, maybe Crenshaw, or Carla, the waitress, would know something about it.

# # #

No one knew Doug Manley's present whereabouts. Standt went through Chris K's contacts at the local DA's office. Manley had been out of touch for almost twenty-four hours, making him essentially AWOL, a fugitive.

Yet, the island had relatively few law enforcement resources, so no one was looking for him at the moment.

Standt was going to start with Doug's brother Brad the following morning. He talked to Chris on the phone and asked him whether he'd contacted Brad.

"No. But I know where he is."

"Where, the surf shop?"

"He's surfing right now, down in Poipu. This is as good a time as any to take a surfing lesson, my friend."

"Are you serious?" Standt ran his hand through his thinning hair, as if to press the fatigue out of his head. He'd had about three and a half hours sleep. The left side of his face still lightly throbbed, and he didn't want to look at it again in the mirror.

At least the shoulder was feeling better; he had a lot of muscle there, from all the weightlifting. It was kind of hard as a rock.

"I'm serious. It's the best way to get to Brad. He's surfing for the next few hours at a place called First Break. I'll come by in my Jeep and pick you up. I have a longboard for you. I'll give you a lesson and we'll talk to Brad…Wear your swim suit and a t-shirt."

Standt had been beaten up, he was under-slept, and now Chris wanted him to play some charade at learning surfing. He took his cell phone, just in case Sam Wilcox called him back.

Then he had a thought. Before Chris showed up with his Jeep, he texted Church: "search this angle: Amanda + Vicodin."

On the other end of the text, Church was on the Lower East Side of Manhattan, still sprawled in bed with iz. Given his Amanda visions the night before in Dos Caminos, he launched into Standt's new directive with an utmost vigor. It felt great to hear from the detective again–he had a purpose once more, beyond just drifting through Manhattan getting high with iz.

iz lived at the center of Church's universe, but hacking for the cops had been his livelihood for the last couple of years. He didn't want to ruin it.

# # #

When Standt met Chris on Kamehameha Drive, the green, mud-caked Wrangler wreaked of weed. The surfer had apparently put himself in the proper frame of mind for riding the waves. A smaller surf board and a ten-foot longboard lay in the open back of the Jeep.

"Did you talk to Brad Manley?" Standt said, faintly annoyed. They were driving along the main highway south.

Chris took his time with the response. He seemed to be already assessing Standt's potential for the waves. Maybe there was something about finding Amanda that must involve a grasp of the Pacific Ocean's subtle metaphysics.

"Yes."

"Does he know where deadbeat Doug is?" He thought "No," but Standt was hoping for a different answer.

"Deadbeat Doug, I like that," Chris said with his calm, beatific grin. "He won't say where he thinks his loser brother is. He's ticked off. He doesn't want to be involved. He just wants to run a surf shop, and surf. I can understand."

"What about Amanda, does he remember her?"

"You'll have to find that out from him. He wasn't in what I'd say a talking mood."

Chris parked the Jeep on the ocean side in Poipu, then unloaded the surfboards. The long yellow one, Standt's, was heavy.

"Do we really have to do this?"

"Listen, you want to talk to Brad, right? This is the proper context, on the water. You're likely to get more out of him. And you really need to get your head straight. You don't look too good. The surfing will do you good. You need some spiritual renewal."

Standt couldn't argue with him on that point.

Chris padded barefoot through the sand, navigating around sun-worshipers stretched out on their towels. Standt followed him, awkwardly lugging the board. It felt like it was made of lead and strained the arm he gripped it with, as well as his back.

"Even investigators have to take time out sometimes," Chris K. called back to him. This was *Hawaii time* again. For Chris, it meant surfing comes first, murder investigations second.

K found a secluded spot and put his board down. Standt willingly dropped his nearby. The fin of the board stuck into the sand with a gritty thud.

"Lie down on the board stomach first," Chris said. "We have to do some dry-land training."

Standt gratefully followed along, because he needed a rest.

"Now get into the push-up position and jump up on the board." Chris demonstrated, then was standing on the board as a surfer would. Left foot first.

Standt leapt up awkwardly on the board, but found that his right foot naturally took the dominant position. Chris K shrugged.

"That's called 'goofy foot.' Now step forward, with the right foot, and pivot." Standt swiveled on the board and promptly tipped over into the sand, thus proving the need for dry-land training.

"Like this," Chris said, "Step forward…pivot." After a couple of self-conscious tries, Standt got it.

"Okay, now stay in that position."

Standt could see a line-up of surfers in the distance, about 300 yards off-shore. They were sitting on their boards in a moderate swell, biding their time. From a distance, it was like watching tall seabirds, and the natural way they bobbed on the surface of the sea.

Chris stood behind him, bent over, and grabbed the back of Standt's surf board. He started to move the board around to simulate the ocean's swell. Standt immediately fell off.

"See. You're out of balance, fundamentally. Now get back on the board, in the same position."

"When do we go in the water?"

"Chill out. Now close your eyes."

"I don't have time for games. We have to find out what happened to Amanda…"

"This is going to help, believe me."

Standt was beaten up, out of balance, and at the mercy of a surfing guru and his "Zen and the Art of Surfing" philosophy. He went along, if only to get this portion of the morning over with so he could investigate Doug Manley.

He closed his eyes. Chris stood beside him and began gently nudging his body in different places. At first, the tyro surfer tottered and tipped off his board. But within minutes his body was making the proper adjustments to Chris' Tai Chi-like pressure points.

"Ah-h, *now* you're getting the hang of it," Chris intoned, ever the encouraging teacher. "See, the whole point of it is, *don't think*. Just go with the flow, literally, beneath the board. Keep your body loosey-goosey. You see, the lawyers, doctors, and engineers I teach surfing to, they have trouble with this point. Get the fundamentals down. But *don't think*. Surfing is not about thinking, it's about feeling, and dialing in."

Right, Standt thought. *Gotcha*. The surfer's advice was just another reminder about how far he was from New York City, for better or worse.

Standt pulled a skin-tight, anti-chafing shirt over his head, then they lugged their boards into the shallow water. A roll of that gut he wasn't proud of stuck out of the bottom of the shirt. He leashed the board to his left ankle with a Velcro loop. Then the board was afloat in front of him as warm salty water washed over his feet from a gentle swell.

He got on the longboard with his toes touching the bottom of it and began to paddle with his hands after Chris.

"Now I can finally accomplish something," Standt thought, knowing that Brad Manley was out there.

Chris looked around at him and smiled. "We're not going to go out to First Break. We're going to try a few small waves first. How do you feel?"

"Wonderful," Standt said ruefully.

The reef was visible about three to four feet below them. Chris had given him a pair of booties to wear on his feet.

"When you fall," Chris said, "just drop off on your side and don't go into the water feet first. You don't want to hit the reef."

They paddled out to where a small swell was breaking. Chris disembarked from his board for a moment and stood up to his chest beside the board.

"I want you to paddle up to me, and I'm going to push you into a few waves. It's a good way to begin."

Standt tried it a few times, to humor Chris, who he needed for an introduction to Brad Manley. As soon as Chris shoved him into a wave, he was able to get to a half-standing position, but then he immediately toppled over into the froth.

As he returned to Chris for another try, the waves smashed him in the face. He was getting it into his eyes and down his throat. He was far from perfecting a technique for working his way back out to the break without getting clobbered.

He was beginning to sense echoes of decades in the past, of frustration and swinging and missing at pitches during a little league game.

"Are we done?" he called out, over the breaking surf.

"You almost have it," Chis said, grinning. "Feet back a little farther…you're not making that first step. Remember. Hop up on to your feet, step forward, and pivot."

Then Standt did it. He felt the wave swell beneath him, and he got up on his feet and stepped forward with his right foot. Pivoted. He was carried away along the top of the water. He heard Chris yell behind him, "Yeahhh!"

Sure, it was a revelation. He felt the cares of the world fall off on either side of him, as though they too were being carried away by the tide. He let the small wave take him all the way to the beach. Then he hopped back on his board and paddled back out to Chris.

"I knew you could do it!"

"Not bad for fifty-two…"

"Not bad. How do you feel?"

"Better. It's something I can tell my son Tim about." He had to get back on the phone soon and catch up with the twelve-year-old.

"Now let's go out and talk with Manley."

Standt had to hand it to Chris. His bout with surfing had cleared his head, settled his frazzled soul. He felt like doing it some more.

Chris began paddling out toward the line-up on First Break. They found Brad Manley, a lean thirty-year-old with long brown hair straddling the back of his surfboard. Manley looked at them, with a surprised annoyance, as Chris and his protege paddled up and settled beside the surfer.

"What's he doing here?" Manley barked. "This is the big leagues."

"He won't be joining the line-up. He's chilling with me."

"As long as your friend knows that this is a loc's break." He pronounced it like "loke."

"Tell him to keep his nose out of it."

With his palms flat on the board and looking bemused, Chris turned to Standt. "The only thing wrong with surfing is surfers. Some of them, they don't have the Aloha Spirit. If you're a kook, and you end up in an advanced break, they'll paddle up and punch you in the nose."

"What's a kook?"

"A beginner, a Barney. Shouldn't be surfing on nothin' but beach break anyways."

Standt looked at Manley, who was watching an athletic female drop into a wave. As the wave crested, she darted up onto the board and was standing in half a blink of an eye. Crouched and concentrated, she descended along the trough of the wave with grace and confidence.

Floating along on his board, Standt glanced back at Manley.

"I'm a detective from New York. I'm looking for your brother."

Manley's eyes narrowed with mild contempt.

"Why don't you just come right to the point?" Chris said facetiously.

"You won't find Doug out here," Manley said, his

eyes following the blond surfer who'd just bailed at the end of her ride.

"Where do you think he is?"

"What's your business with him?"

"I'm looking for Amanda Wilcox."

"Oh. Before you ask the question, I rented the board to her. I feel really bad about what happened. She was a nice chick. *Real* nice. Whatever happened to her, she didn't deserve it. Maybe she shouldn't have gone out alone on her board. But we don't deny someone a rental because they want to paddle alone in the middle of a calm day. They sign the waiver, we rent the equipment. I hope they find out what happened to her. Shine some light on what happened. Hell…maybe she's still alive somewhere…maybe."

"Was she with anybody at the time, in your shop?"

"No. It was routine. Doug didn't have anything to do with her."

"Why did he run away? I know he's in trouble. But where would he go, here on Kauai? Doesn't he know he's making more trouble for himself? It seems like an admission of guilt if you flee…"

Brad Manley began paddling away. He looked over his shoulder.

"Look, I don't have much to do with my brother these days. I gave him a job, but I can't keep him out of trouble." Apparently, Standt thought, he wasn't his brother's keeper.

"And now I'm not going to take anymore questions. I'm going to surf."

"You know, he might be in better shape getting found by me than the cops or the feds," Standt called out after the surfer. "All I want to know is, if he ran into Amanda in the countryside. He's in big trouble with the feds if he's gone off island."

Manley floated on his board for a moment and looked at Standt with an air of knowing impatience. "Doug isn't off Kauai. He's north," he said, with a subtle nod toward the mountains. "Somewhere in the bush."

Standt watched Manley paddle away and edge into the front of the line-up. He turned to Chris, who still straddled his board, bobbing up and down and trailing his fingers in the blue-green water.

"What are you going to do now?"

"I'm going to wait–and catch a wave in." Chris had naturally dark skin tanned copper, and knotty muscles. He had let his stomach go though, an old surfer who didn't deny himself the pleasures of Hawaii.

Standt thought again about the diversity of unseen wildlife beneath his board. A man had been attacked by a tiger shark in these waters within the year. A wave bucked over his board and knocked him into the water. But he quickly recovered and scrambled back aboard. He could see the darkly furrowed reef beneath the transparent, frothy, sun-infused water.

The sun scorched his back, even covered by the shirt, and the scruff of his neck. "I'm going back in."

When he returned to the sand he beached the board and aimed quickly for the bag of belongings he'd left by a blanket. He was afraid they'd be stolen, or at least rifled through, but he found his cell phone intact.

He had a return call from Sam Wilcox.

CHAPTER 25: SAM

"Did Amanda have a problem with Vicodin?"

Chris had dropped off the detective at the Princeville condo, then drove off to, no doubt, snag a nap at his Hanalei bungalow. Standt had his surfing memories but was no closer to finding Doug Manley.

He'd reached Sam Wilcox on his cell phone while standing on the grassy bluff and gazing out toward the North Pacific. The topic of Vicodin couldn't be avoided; he understood it would be a sensitive one with the old man.

"A problem? What do you mean?" Sam had a crack in his voice and was speaking from a New York City law office.

"I have reason to believe she had an interest in exploring Vicodin addiction treatment. There were a lot of Web searches."

"Is that all? Web searches?" Wilcox acted defensive, predictably.

"It's worth it to explore that angle. One thing can lead

to another…"

"Okay. Understood." Standt sensed the resistance drop in Sam's voice. It was a heretofore unrevealed dark corner of Amanda's psyche. "She was a dancer in New York. It was one of her loves. She injured her back. She told me about it. She had to take Vicodin for the pain."

"When did this happen?"

"About three weeks before she left for Kauai. So why is this relevant, detective?"

"Do you happen to know whether she had a problem with them? The meds?"

"My daughter wasn't a drug addict. She viewed her body as a temple."

"I'm aware of that." She might have partied though, a bit, he thought. The "tabloid garbage" that Katie had mentioned; at times, where there's smoke there's fire.

Standt had texted Church hours before and asked him to explore Kauai's pharmacies, every CVS and Walgreens, for evidence of Vicodin prescriptions made out under Amanda's name. So far the hacker hadn't found anything. Standt had searched himself for local drug-treatment centers and had a call into one of them. Nothing yet.

There was a pause and some silence on the phone line. Then an audible sigh from Wilcox.

"Amanda called me once, a couple of months ago. It was at night. She said she was having a little problem with the painkillers. They're *very* addictive. She'd been through a difficult week, but she had a handle on it. She found it a little upsetting, she was used to being clean and totally in control of her physical life. She's a health-oriented person.

"It just snuck up on her, and I'm glad she confided in me. I gave her the name of my physician in Manhattan, for a referral. And that was that. It's my understanding that it was never a severe problem, and was eventually solved. So now you know. I don't think it had anything to do with what happened on the paddleboard that day…"

"I'm not suggesting she was impaired, sir. I'm wondering if she got involved, inadvertently, with a distributor. An illegal one. It's one of the options I'm exploring."

He didn't want to suggest to Wilcox that his daughter got in with the criminal element, and was essentially a junkie who brought misfortune upon herself. But…he did want to unravel this Vicodin thread.

"That's all I need, for now," Standt said.

Wilcox's voice now had a blunt, harder edge. "Do you know what happened to my daughter, detective?"

Standt paused, because he knew Wilcox was leaning on him given the slow pace of his investigation. Standt had been on Kauai about a week. He'd gotten stoned and gone surfing…

"She did not die of drowning or a shark attack. Of that I'm about ninety-five percent certain. So your initial skepticism was spot on. The board itself appears doctored, to make it appear like a shark fatality. We just don't know who's responsible for that yet."

"Who are your primary suspects? Who are you focusing on now?" Standt felt himself on the stand.

"I'm pursuing two threads now–one involving Monsanto, and…"

"Monsanto?" Wilcox scoffed. "What could they possibly have to do with Amanda?"

His disbelief was palpable, as though doubting Standt's competence. The Wilcox's of the world were used to getting what they want, and quickly. The old gentlemanly demeanor seemed to have evaporated.

"Amanda, as you know, was at the center of anti-GMO protests. It's very convenient for Monsanto to have her out of the way."

"To the extent of *killing* her? That's preposterous! They're a hardball corporation, but not the Sicilian Mafia."

"Really?" Standt felt like saying. He decided not to bring up the Bruno pay-off angle, because he was beginning to lose interest and confidence in that angle anyways. It would just make this a more difficult conversation than it already was.

He wondered if Wilcox was about to fire him. He supposed it would be justified. It would not be beneficial for Standt's pride or freelance career, but Wilcox would handle it according to the precepts of noblesse oblige, by paying Standt in full.

Standt was beginning to feel very crappy, until he remembered what the grizzled reporter Don Latham told him once. Whenever you're stressing out about something that isn't important in the larger scheme of things, remember that we could be all dead in a month from an asteroid strike or a plague. Or a similar calamity. It could all be over soon. So don't forget to enjoy life and put it all into perspective; take it a day at a time.

Standt kept plugging along on the phone: "Another thread I'm following is the reason I asked you this question in the first place. Maybe Amanda hadn't locked into a good treatment program yet and needed one more prescription and didn't have a doctor handy on Kauai. It can be hard to get a doctor to renew prescriptions for Vicodin.

"The people who sell bootleg prescriptions usually are not nice people. And since Amanda has disappeared under suspicious circumstances, I would be remiss if I didn't investigate that angle. Did Amanda need to obtain Vicodin, and if so, who was she getting it from?"

Wilcox paused for another moment, to the point that Standt thought he'd lost the connection. Then the older man was back on.

"For the sake of argument, although I think your theory is a stretch, who do *you* think she was getting her prescriptions on Kauai from?"

"There's a person involved with drug distribution on Kauai named Doug Manley, and there's too much circumstantial evidence surrounding him and Amanda to ignore a possible link."

"If it's only circumstantial or tangential, why bother?"

Remember? Standt thought. You were the one who hired me to pick apart the glaring flaws in the official theories on this case.

"Because I've found over time that sometimes it's the circumstantial evidence that's staring you in the face, that's just the thing you're looking for. The thing that solves a case."

There was no response.

"Mr. Wilcox?"

"Yes."

"I'm leaving no stone unturned."

"Suit yourself. Let me know what you find." Then abruptly Wilcox hung up.

CHAPTER 26: BACK TO CARLA

Standt didn't get an answer on his cell phone when he tried to call Carla, so he decided to go straight back to the St. Regis and find her.

Just when he had valet-parked his car–all he had to do is tip the driver five bucks–his cell phone chimed. It was the waitress.

"I've been meaning to get back in touch with you," she said.

"*Perfect* timing. Are you working now on the terrace?"

"Yeah. But I can get off for fifteen minutes. The rush hasn't started yet." It wasn't near to four p.m.

"Can I meet you down by the beach, where they rent the stuff?"

"In five minutes."

"Okay."

Standt took the long flight of stairs through the groaning bamboo groves, with leaves and small crushed bananas scattered about the steps. When he got down to the beach, he saw Carla standing and smoking a cigarette in the shade of a palm tree.

Standt removed his shoes, placed sunglasses on to the top of his nose, and walked across the sand.

"You know, you shouldn't do that."

"What, smoke? I know," she said, and dropped the cigarette perfunctorily, stubbing it with a black shoe on a sandy, concrete path.

"I guess everybody tells you that but they miss the point."

Carla cocked her head at him. "And what would that be?"

"That a person needs a cigarette sometimes. That life has bumps along the road."

She nodded. "I should quit anyways. It's always tomorrow, or next week."

"We made a connection. I was just trying to call you. I had questions, and you wanted to tell me something about Amanda."

"I think she was in trouble. No, I should say, I *know* she was in trouble."

"What kind?"

"She had an argument, up on the terrace. Pardon my French, but you're the New York cop right? She was hanging out with one of the assholes here at the St. Regis bar. We get them once in a while. They wash in on the tide, from the sailboats and yachts, humanity's pampered flotsam and jetsam."

"What's his name?"

She'd looked at one of his credit-card statements.

"Henry, or Hank, Crenshaw."

The name was familiar to Standt, but he didn't grab on to it right away. Fatigue, its dregs clouding his mind.

"Amanda would never hang around with his type. *Ever.*" Carla was standing angrily, with her arms crossed. "Something was happening that was *making* her hang with him. I think she was in trouble, as I said. Then this really grungy, floozy type comes on to the patio to meet them. Lousy clothes; she was wasted. Carrying a paper bag."

"What was in the bag? Drugs?"

"Didn't get to see it, but it wasn't liquor. She gave it to Amanda. Amanda took it like it was something she needed, but despised. She wasn't happy with herself. Then they had a little fight and the…" Carla looked around her for prying ears. "…douchebag tried to drag her off the patio."

"What happened to the floozy?"

"She laughed like a twit and left."

"Had you ever seen her before?"

"Never."

"What do *you* think it was all about?"

"It couldn't be about anything but drugs. Maybe Amanda had a coke problem, or worse, although she didn't look like it. Never looked like it. Maybe she took a wrong turn."

Things were beginning to take shape, just when Standt was feeling oppressed by the island's humid torpor. The Tropic Of Cancer climate had not necessarily agreed with him.

"Amanda had a problem with Vicodin," Standt explained. "She got injured dancing in New York, then got hooked on the pills. So possibly she was getting a delivery of the stuff…" He gazed at the water, where Amanda was last seen, and let his mind connect the missing pieces.

"Or methadone, or something like that. Another opiate," Carla said.

"How do you know about that?"

"My Auntie had a Vicodin problem, and they gave

her methadone to ween her off it."

"Methadone…when did this happen with the loser and Amanda on the patio?"

"It was the last time I saw her before she disappeared. Maybe a week before. So it had to have been…about three weeks ago." It helped to remember that she'd suffered about three weeks of insomnia since that afternoon, as well.

"Did you tell anyone else about the confrontation, like Bruno Reilly?"

"He never asked."

"Somehow that doesn't surprise me. Thank you Carla. Thanks for telling me."

"I wish I'd done more," Carla said, then a tear streaked down her cheek, and she reached up to wipe it away. She fell against Standt and pressed her face against his shoulder, where she sobbed and unburdened herself.

"I hope something hasn't happened to Amanda," she cried. "I really wanted to say something before. I really did. She was so nice to me. I'll never forgive myself. Poor Amanda…she didn't deserve this. Get 'em…get 'em, who did this!" Carla's sudden snarl betrayed an abusive past, until she just as instantly drifted back to sadness.

Standt gently nudged her off his shoulder and held her. "You've told me more valuable stuff than anyone on Kauai so far. You did your job."

She cracked a smile through the tears. "I've been smoking like a chimney, drinking like a fish, since this happened."

Then it dawned on him. Dash Crenshaw, the Manhattan boyfriend, with the same last name. He struck his forehead with the palm of his hand. Standt turned away from Carla to mount the steps and dial Crenshaw's number, when his cell phone buzzed.

It was Chris Keʻ alohilani. He told Standt that female

remains had been found on Hideaways Beach. He told him where that was. Standt didn't say anything to Carla. He started to breath hard and felt like sprinting. His heart pounded; a sweat broke out on his brow.

He let the phone down and turned away from Carla with a fake, half smile. He walked up the white, sandy beach, ablaze with Kauai's sun, beneath the St. Regis, to clamor over the peninsula and reach Hideaways on the other side.

CHAPTER 27: REMAINS

Standt had seen it all before, or thought he did. When he walked across the black lava rocks to reach Hideaways, he emerged from some trees and recognized, right away, the somber assemblage of professionals who commonly attend to the discovery of human remains.

They stood near a little circle of hastily erected yellow warning tape.

Off to the side were a couple of traumatized snorkelers who couldn't tear themselves away from the scene. One of Bruno's deputies was there. An EMT, the county coroner, and a *Garden Island* reporter with her photographer were also part of the group.

The young, eager-beaver writer stood about ten feet away from the focus of everyone's attention looking awestruck and taking notes, but they weren't letting her any closer.

Chris K walked down the beach from the opposite

direction. He waved Standt over. He'd give the detective access to the remains. Not that Standt could draw any conclusion from what he saw.

The remains had been washed up onto the black rocks and exposed to the morning sun, so a putrid smell arose from them. Standt had been around for many a fishing-out of bloated bodies from the Hudson and East Rivers, but he'd never seen a body that had been actively fed upon by several different species, including the birds and crabs. The fetid pile of water-logged skin, bones, and clothing were twisted, gouged, pockmarked, and barely recognizable as human.

The coroner and his female assistant were in the process of bagging them. Standt saw sand-encrusted, bunched-up and damp long hair but he did not allow his eyes to rest too long upon the skull and torso. He noticed tattered blue cloth among the remains.

"Do they have a good DNA lab here?" He doubted it.

"It will have to be sent off island to Honolulu," Chris said, turning away from the smell and the scene with a disgusted expression and gazing out at the flat ocean.

They hadn't mentioned Amanda yet, but they were both hoping for the same thing, that it wasn't her but some stranger who'd toppled off a boat or cruise ship. Yet, that person too had a dad, mom, grandparents, and his or her own life tragically cut short.

"There are no other missing female reports?"

"Nothing. Nothing yet."

In his detective days, Standt used to carry scented tissues for just this purpose. This time he took his shirt off and held it over his face. He wanted one more look. He put his glasses on, exchanged a knowing look with the coroner, and bent down to inspect the remains closer.

He saw the blue-jean clothing, bound up with the awful gray porridge to which the sea had converted the corpse. But he didn't see anything like black booties or bathing-suit material.

Standt wore a grimace when he lifted the shirt away from his face. He backed off and spoke again to Chris.

"She was wearing booties when she went out on the board. Tethered to a leash. I don't see anything like that here. And it seems to have…a dungaree material. The remains aren't near old enough. These aren't ten-day-old remains."

"They *could* be…"

"I'd bet they're not. We didn't get any worthwhile DNA from the paddleboard, but we will from her clothing left in her apartment."

"Not only that," Standt added, "but the location. The remains washed up on a different beach than the board."

"She could have been separated from her board. She might have unfastened the leash–we don't know," Chris said, scratching his goatee with his arms crossed. "But I'm with you on this one. We shouldn't be too quick to assume this…" he cleared his throat weakly. "…is Amanda, just because she's the only missing person."

Maybe there was a cold case involving a woman missing on Kauai that Chris didn't know about?

Standt was going to contact Wilcox, tell him about the finding, but leaven the news with his own opinion that the remains most likely weren't his daughter's. Sam was going to find out about this anyways, via media reports. Wilcox and his assistants had to provide the clothing and DNA sample for comparison's sake.

But if it wasn't Amanda, they had to properly identify the body, or Standt's opinion wasn't worth much.

At any rate, the DNA results wouldn't come in for about a week, and only if they were lucky.

Standt put his shirt back on, donned his sunglasses, and walked back down the small beach with Chris and up the steep path to the surfer's car.

"You can tell me everything they find out from those remains, right?"

"Yeah. As soon as it comes in."

Standt paused in front of the open Jeep door.

"How often does this happen on Kauai? They find remains but there's no link yet with accidents or drownings?"

"Almost never," Chris said, with a melancholy, a regret, that was unusual for him. "Kauai's a special place. An island apart. We don't have stuff like this happen, Amanda disappearing, nightmare remains on the beach. It isn't a city. This is why people come here. This isn't the Hawaii I grew up in. What's happening to Kauai?"

Chris left the question dangling, then slammed the driver door shut. Maybe bad GMO DNA had contaminated the tropical constitution of the place, Standt thought.

\# # #

Chris dropped Standt off at the Princeville condo. He found Katie writing on her laptop outside. He could tell she had been crying. He had already texted her about the corpse washed up on Hideaways.

"Was it her?" she said. "Tell me it wasn't."

"It wasn't. I mean, if I was a betting man…the remains aren't old enough. They were in rough shape, granted. Probably some of the most degraded I've ever seen. I've found skeletons, but in terms of remains that still involved skin and…"

"Alright alright, spare me the gross details. Please."

"You asked…"

"Church is trying to get ahold of you."

"How do you know?"

"I got an email from him. Contact him ASAP."

Standt read the email message. Church had found a historical record on Hank Crenshaw by searching the internet archives. If this was the same Crenshaw. Standt called the hacker back on his cell phone. It had seemed like days since they'd spoken.

"Where are you?" It suddenly occurred to Standt that having Church present on Kauai might make a difference. You can't accomplish *everything* remotely.

"Brooklyn."

"What do you have?"

"Henry is a bad boy. He's been in trouble for a long time. If it's the same guy. I found some old articles online."

"What did he do?"

"He went to…Boston College. 2002. Another student fell off a roof during a party. He was suspected of pushing him. But they didn't have enough evidence on him and the case against him was tossed. Then a girl charged him with rape. They finally kicked him out of college."

"Does he have a prison record?"

"No. He had a cocaine charge a couple years later but Daddy's lawyers got him off."

"Does he have a brother named Dash?"

Church paused. "I found them on one of those people search web sites. Yeah. He does."

Then it has to be the same Crenshaw. Standt was looking forward to *that* conversation.

Church had the usual guttural, just-woke-up tone on the phone. "Another thing. Some of those cell numbers you gave me. The ones calling in over and over to Amanda. They were from Hank Crenshaw on Kauai. Then two calls from Doug Manley."

"Give me Crenshaw's address on the island." Standt knew Church would have it.

Standt and Chris K drove together to Crenshaw's house. It was in Hanalei Town, several blocks back from the beach. Wet clouds hung over the beach, weighing down the trees with their huge, moist leaves. The heavy, saturated air made Standt feel limp and enervated.

The small bungalow was almost hidden in a riot of undergrowth and weeds. They made their way down a narrow path with wild chickens poking around in the soggy leaves.

A sleepy roommate answered their knock on the front door of the bungalow, but he hadn't seen Crenshaw in three days. He had a scraggly red goatee, a t-shirt with yellowed armpits, and flowered shorts that resembled boxers. Standt looked past him along a dirty, fraying rug into the grubby, murky interior of a slovenly bachelor's pad.

Standt felt like barging inside and searching Crenshaw's room, but they didn't have a search warrant. The roommate, who said he cut fish at The Dolphin Center and surfed his boogie board, didn't seem suspicious, only hungover and not up to much.

Standt had already called Crenshaw's cell phone. Henry had a perfunctory recorded message: "I'm not here. Leave a message." Standt didn't expect to hear back from him. He did tell Church to try to hack into AT&T or Verizon phone records for any sign that Crenshaw was making phone calls in the last few days.

Both Manley and Crenshaw were essentially fugitives–Crenshaw because he'd had a confrontation with Amanda before she disappeared. Chris used his local and federal contacts to make sure that the two hadn't fled from Lihue Airport. There were no records of any departing flights with either of them as passengers.

Standt suspected Crenshaw might be in the same local vicinity as Manley. They both had called Amanda during the week before she disappeared, so something fishy was in the works.

Standt was antsy and wanted to mount a physical search for Manley and Crenshaw, right away.

"When?" Chris drove the Jeep in the direction of Princeville.

"Now–and I need a gun."

"I don't know about that," Chris shook his head. "I doubt you're permitted in Hawaii for a weapon. Am I right?"

"I'm a permitted peace officer in the United States. That's all that matters. This case is getting hot right now and…where do you keep *your* gun?"

Standt didn't believe that Chris, despite his ultra-mellow vibe, would never have a need for a firearm.

"The glove compartment," Chris said.

Standt opened it up and was pleasantly surprised to find his personal model beneath the registration and other documents, a Beretta Compact 9mm.

He pulled it out and inspected it. "Not everyone on Kauai is totally mellow." He thought of Bruno Reilly in passing.

Chris flashed a look at him as the Jeep's tires spun out on the gravelly pavement. "You could really get me in deep shit if you got caught using that…"

"It's time to get our feet and hands dirty," Standt said, ignoring the surfer's admonishment. "Let's go into the bush. You got a map? Let's find Manley and Crenshaw. They had something going together on Amanda. I know it. They could get off Kauai any moment. By boat."

"Wait. Hold your horses. I'm not ready to do that now."

"What, you want to go surfing first? I don't have all the time in the world. Listen, if it's about wages, consider what you're being paid by Sam Wilcox. We're both on the payroll. He pays well too. You're on the same gravy train with me. And he's going to be mighty happy if we find out what happened to his daughter."

"We can't just go banging around in the bush right now. We need a plan. Kauai isn't a small place." They were almost to the exit into Kamehameha Road.

"Cambodia. That place your friend showed us. In the helicopter. Let's drive in there. I have a feeling they're in there. My gut tells me that. It's not too big a place, and it must have only a few roads." They *were* in a Jeep, Standt thought. There's nothing back there this vehicle won't be able to handle. And they're armed. This was the time to go into the bush after Crenshaw and Manley.

"How do you know they're in there, other than your gut…your visions?" Chris had pulled the Jeep over to the side of the road near the statuesque fountain at the entrance to Princeville.

"Aren't visions essential to *you*? Your spiritual vibes, after you get high?"

Chris didn't really have an answer for that.

"If I don't pursue this one, and if Amanda's case goes cold on us, I'll forever regret it. *We'll* forever regret it. I can't tell you how many cases I made progress on after a hunch…"

"Okay. Okay." Chris pulled back out into the highway.

"We go into the bush."

CHAPTER 28: SUBMERGED

Standt reached Dash Crenshaw when they were in the Jeep.

They were driving on a rutted dirt road through an old coffee and pineapple plantation that had been abandoned and given over to weeds and long grasses.

"I want to ask you a few things about your brother Henry," Standt said.

"Hank?" Then Crenshaw was silent for what seemed like an eternity. Finally, his voice crackled over a flawed connection. Dash was in Manhattan, walking down Park Avenue at 50th Street. Dealmaking in Standt's old Midtown police beat.

"I haven't seen him in a while. We haven't talked."

"He's been on Kauai, during the time Amanda was here."

"I knew that."

"How come you didn't mention it to me, that time at

the diner?"

"I didn't think it was relevant."

"It is now. It was then."

"How do you mean?"

Standt wondered what kind of day it was in Manhattan. He thought of a sunny walk up to Central Park with his son, Tim.

"What's the weather?" Standt asked.

"What?"

"Is it nice right now, where you are?"

Dash didn't answer for several seconds, suggesting he paid no attention to weather patterns, the difference between sun, clouds, and fog, unless someone forced him to.

"It's sunny. Breezy."

Perfect, Standt thought, and a smile worked its way across a face taut with fatigue. He was in Hawaii, but he missed New York.

"Your brother was hanging out with Amanda just a few days before she disappeared. And she didn't look happy to be with him, a witness told me. They were fighting. Now your brother's been gone for three days. Did he ever get arrested for drug dealing in Hawaii?"

"I don't know. No. Not that I know of."

"How well did he know Amanda?"

Another meaningful pause, then he said noncommittally: "They knew each other pretty well."

"What is it you're not telling me?" Crenshaw couldn't wriggle out of this one.

He cleared his throat. Standt heard a siren and the tidal rush of street noise from Crenshaw's end.

"Amanda went out with Hank before me."

Now Standt was silent. He looked out the window at the thickening brush and the clouds of red dust Chris' Jeep had kicked up behind them. They bounced along the rough, backcountry road with Standt pressing the phone to his ear.

"How long ago?"

"Eighteen months, two years ago. They met in New York."

"Let me guess, Amanda ended it." How could Amanda have ended up with Hank the Knife?

"Yes."

"Did Henry follow her out to Kauai?"

"No. I mean…he might have." His voice betrayed a stumbling hesitancy. "Listen detective, I have to go now. I have a meeting."

Chris had pulled the Jeep over to the side of the road.

"How did Amanda ever end up with your brother in the first place?"

"He gave to one of her fundraisers. Then she went to a few shows and operas with him."

"So he's ticked off at you for going out with her?"

"I have to go. I'm going to try to call him this morning. Find out where he is. If I find out anything, I'll call you right back." Then he hung up. Standt put his phone away. Chris stood beside the Jeep at the roadside.

Before Standt got out of the car, he took the Beretta out of the glove compartment. He shoved it into a deep pocket on the side of a roomy pair of cargo pants he wore.

"Is this loaded?" he asked Chris.

"Yeah, but the safety's on."

"Do you have any other ammunition?"

"Under the passenger seat."

Standt reached beneath the seat and removed a magazine, stashing that in the same pocket as the pistol.

"You're not going to use that weapon," the surfer said warily. "You're not going turn into the loose cannon on Kauai."

"It's insurance. I have a feeling Manley has friends in

here, and they carry more than spears."

Chris shook his head, with an air of "What have I gotten myself into?"

# # #

The red, gritty dirt road was barely wide enough for one vehicle. It was silent, humid, and windless.

Standt looked up. They were close to the flanks of the huge, forbidding mountain with its permanent crown of dark clouds–Mount Waialeale. He reached into a front pocket for a pair of sunglasses. When he put them on, they lent the illusion that he was cooler. They stood on the roadside beneath the relentless equatorial sun.

On either side of the road was a tangle of weeds and vegetation leading down steeply to a swampy wetlands. Standt started to walk. He had his cell phone, wallet, and Beretta, but not much else.

"What do you want to do?" Chris called after him.

"I'm going to scope out this area. Ask around for Manley and Crenshaw."

"You're not going to find much. It's just old plantations, a few roads and paths, maybe a couple of shacks. It's Cambodia. You're not quite in the middle of it, but almost. This road will give out soon. It's a dead end."

"Then we'll turn around. Are you coming?"

"I think not. I think I'll stay with the Jeep. You have a cell phone? Is it charged up?"

"Yeah."

"Don't get lost!"

"I'm just going to ask anyone I run into if they've seen these two hombres." Then Standt headed down the path alone, feeling around reassuringly for the weapon.

In a few minutes he'd left Chris' Jeep behind. Above him was a vault of old hardwood trees, and beneath that, the path was choked with ferns and dead leaves and banana trees strangled by vines.

Sweat ran down the back of his neck; he reached down and scratched his shoulder blade and felt the soaked back of his shirt. Mosquitos swarmed in front of his face. He should have brought some water. He looked behind him; the red-dirt path disappeared amidst the vines, tall grasses, and suffocating vegetation.

Standt still had a lot of narrow road left in front of him. He'd gone past the old plantation and into "the bush."

He looked at his watch. If he didn't see anything for half an hour he'd turn around. He felt around for the cell phone; he sensed the handgun's weight knocking against the side of his leg. He looked up again and the dead, drooping foliage was so thick that it blocked any view of the mountain's dense flanks.

It almost blocked out the sun. He wasn't on Kauai's beaches anymore.

\# # #

Church was taking Airtrain from New York to John F. Kennedy International Airport. He had a small backpack with a laptop, a change of clothes, a cell phone, and his Kauai plane tickets.

Standt had always told him, "You have a hunch, you can break a case, then don't hesitate; use the credit card I gave you and get your ass on a plane."

This was the first time he had actually done that. He was in the middle of what was probably the most publicized and notorious missing-person's case in the world. He knew more about it than most people; probably only Standt knew more.

The different names and their implicit unsavoriness swirled around in his head: Doug Manley, Hank Crenshaw,

Bruno Reilly. He knew them only as numbers, cell phones, accounts, Web addresses, all tied to strangers who steal, kill, grasp for and seize what they think is theirs.

Standt didn't know the latest piece of information that Church had picked up. But he hadn't returned Church's latest cell-phone call. That sealed the deal and Church bought the plane tickets.

He knew it had to be relevant. If he had learned anything from the middle-aged detective it was, trust your instincts, your gut.

Church had hacked into Verizon's and AT&T's cell-phone exchanges and servers on Kauai and the rest of Hawaii. He pulled an all-nighter and swung a large net. That's why the National Security Agency did what they did; they grabbed tens of millions of web searches, phone conversations, and text messages, hoping they'd find some nuggets amid the millions of bits of dross and the accumulated tailings.

Illegal? Yes. But it had a certain wisdom. They wouldn't have done it if it hadn't been successful in the past. The spooks even had a name for it, looking for certain patterns within giant clusters of indiscriminate data. "Chatter." A certain amplitude of messaging among potential bad guys meant something malevolent was building in the atmosphere.

When the chatter reached a certain intensification, the warnings came out. Church could be a spook if he ever wanted to.

He'd searched the chatter in Kauai, once he'd felt that the phone calls from Manley and Crenshaw had already given him all that he would get from them.

The data included a random text message issuing from a private number somewhere inland on Kauai. Not from Amanda's cell phone. When he read it his mind exploded:

"help me a.w."

CHAPTER 29: CAMBODIA

Standt was alone on this jungle trail. He saw what looked like a few driveways. He walked down one of them, but it ended in a pile of vegetative debris and toppled down banana trees. It was as if the density of the underbrush, all the impenetrable dead wood and leaves and ferns and vine-entwined tree trunks that blocked out the sun, had discouraged even the most determined builder.

There was nothing very habitable in the immediate surroundings. It was an easy region to hide in.

Man had mostly given this part of the island back to Kauai. Standt certainly saw no sign of sophisticated drug operations. This was where he could use that helicopter and about two dozen other men, to fan out on these remote Kauai slopes and search for the fugitives.

Just when he was going to give up and turn around he saw a man walking ahead up the trail in the same direction.

He was a tiny older guy with skinny, sunburned legs,

sandals, and long hair and beard. He wore a floppy bush hat and carried a walking stick and a small rucksack. He looked like a hippy. He seemed lost in his thoughts and the detective startled him.

"Excuse me, do you live here?"

"Yeah, near here." The man glared fearfully at Standt, then his face seemed to break in an instant and he smiled and showed wide gaps in his teeth. He seemed at least sixty, or more. His humble appearance suggested the same surrender to the intimidating riot of vegetation.

"Do you know Doug Manley?"

The man adjusted his hat and scratched his head.

"Can't recall him."

"What about Hank Crenshaw?"

"No. Never heard of him. Sorry. We don't have addresses back here. Or neighborhoods, in the way you usually think of them." Then he smiled again.

Standt looked around. "Where are the homes back here?"

The man looked wary again. He leaned on his stick.

"No houses, really. It's bungalows, falling-down ones usually. Old barracks from the plantations. A few live in those. Even tents." He stuck his chin out towards the flanks of the mountains. "You'd never find my shack. You'd have to know where it is beforehand. I like it that way."

Standt fished around in his pocket for his old NYPD badge. He had to get the old codger's attention.

Flashing the badge, he said: "I'm looking for those two guys because they're on the run from the law."

The old man swallowed and the Adam's Apple of his thin neck bobbed up and down.

"I'm not surprised. 'Aint much law up here. Just people, minding their own business. Survivin' on the island."

"How long have you been here?"

"Oh, since '69. Came back from 'Nam and decided to live out my life on Kauai."

"Vietnam…do you know why they call this Cambodia?"

"Who calls it that?"

"Some people I work with. It's a reference to remoteness, I gather. The heat. Maybe a reference to Cambodia and 'Nam, as a place people go to where they don't belong. Where they weren't supposed to be."

The man leaned off his stick, like he was ready to go.

"Nah, I've been to real Cambodia. Those are good people. Gentle. Except for that horror show after the war. Generally real nice people. This is nothing like Cambodia. I gotta go. Hope you find who're you're lookin' for."

"Do you know of any houses, or shacks, that seem to have a lot of activity? People hanging around, going back and forth, a lot of vehicle traffic?"

"No traffic here, none whatsoever."

"I mean greater than usual."

"You might try at the end of this path. Then there's a small clearing on the right. Back in there."

"How far?"

"About a mile; mile and a half. I've seen settlements up there. Don't tell 'em I told yah. I don't want anyone mad at me. I've lived here for more than forty years and I don't plan on leaving. Fact is, I've nowhere else to go."

"Mum's the word."

The man nodded, adjusted the bush hat, then kept on going up the road, at a faster pace, like he didn't want to accompany Standt.

The detective got out his cell phone and put in a call to Chris, but the surfer didn't answer. Then he started walking again, maybe one hundred yards behind the old man.

The old veteran kept looking behind him, to see if

Standt was still there. Then when Standt came to a bend in the road, he found that the man had simply vanished. He had disappeared into a small parting of the weeds, ferns, and jungle riot.

He was right; he couldn't be followed, unless one had a machete and some feel for jungle tracking.

Standt kept going along the hot, windless path until he arrived at the subtle clearing in the brush that the old man had told him about.

# # #

Katie had stayed behind in Princeville. She'd taken numerous photos for her article, of Hanalei Bay and the St. Regis and sunsets and the beaches where Amanda was last seen or rumored to have recently been to.

Katie was planning on leaving the island with the mostly written article, larded with intrigue, including the discovery of the remains on the beach, when she found out from one of her *Slate* colleagues in Manhattan that Turner Espray was coming to Kauai.

The actress had read the rumors about her friend Amanda. She'd read about the case that had come apart at the seams. She wanted to use her own formidable influence and resources to shed light on a tragedy that still haunted her.

She was going to show up on the island with lawyers and bodyguards. *Lawyers, guns, and money*...Katie thought from the old song lyrics.

Amanda had been one of her best friends. Turner, though unmarried, was planning on asking Amanda to be her head bridesmaid, when and if she ever settled on one man.

A tabloid press report said that Turner was supposed to be staying at a private rented villa in Kilauea, Kauai. That sealed the deal for Katie. She cancelled her return flight and held on to the article.

Her employers didn't care; they wanted this new wrinkle added to the story. Turner Espray and the Hollywood/Manhattan connection to the rescue.

On one of Standt and Katie's first dates, they had seen the actress live on the Broadway stage. They had sat in first-row orchestra seats, a big splurge for Standt. Turner was playing Maggie in Tennessee William's *Cat On A Hot Tin Roof.*

Standt was riveted by the actress's verve, energy, and the sexuality she brought to the already steamy part. Katie was amused. She respected the willingness of a budding film star to tackle a classic role on stage. Turner was only in her late twenties.

At one point, when delivering a passionate monologue in a small dress that showed off her curves, she fixed Standt with a stare. His heart raced, and the man who had faced gangsters and whackos on more than one occasion, finally looked away in embarrassment.

He couldn't believe he had done that. He couldn't sustain eye contact with the beautiful Turner, even when she wanted to. Only his male ego made that a special moment in his life, as Turner almost certainly forgot it within seconds, or had never really noticed him in the first place.

When Turner arrived, her presence on Kauai was no longer rumor. It became another one of the island's circus-like sideshows. *People* magazine's web site, then the *Huffington Post* and *Slate* picked up on the story, followed by dozens of trite Hollywood tabloids. A few paparazzis had showed up on the beaches, as though looking for a Facebook party.

Maybe that's why she had chosen an out-of-the-way villa instead of swanky digs like the St. Regis Hotel–she wanted anonymity.

The other effect of Espray's arrival is that it rekindled the interest surrounding Amanda's disappearance, just when it had lost its mojo.

Espray had placed a call to detective Standt, as she stood on a 500-foot lanai looking out at the sea, but as he was wandering unguided through the jungle.

He'd turned off his cell phone to conserve battery power. It now lay in his pocket and contained Turner's unheard message as he fought his way through Kauai's undergrowth at the foot of Mount Waialeale.

CHAPTER 30: SHADOWS OF THE JUNGLE

Standt found himself in a clearing surrounded by the tangled undergrowth that crept up the trunks of the old bent-over hardwoods and strangled the greenness out of them. The vegetation itself seemed insatiable, as if it would consume him as well as the trees.

Chris hadn't answered his cell phone call, but Standt couldn't stop himself. He had to see this search through to its logical conclusion.

At least, if he found out who lived in this so-called "settlement," and it turned out to be no one of interest, then they could cross out this particular route in "Cambodia."

He found tire ruts in the tall grasses. He followed them. They looked like the tracks of a four-wheel drive vehicle, digging large divots in the now muddy ground. They led to a larger clearing in the jungle.

He had now soaked through his entire shirt. He took it off and wrapped it around his sunglasses on his head. His mouth was pasty, and he spat the sticky white saliva into a pile of dead leaves. He felt around for his pistol again, but he didn't want to display it, yet.

He didn't want to shock anyone he would come upon by mistake. At the moment, he was a sorry sight. His upper body was marked by patches of sun-burned skin. Sweat poured off his brow. The heavy torpid air provided no relief.

He kept marching up what turned into a trail.

It widened, then a space through the overgrowth proffered a view of at least three structures. They had small roofs and big verandas that stuck out of the trees and bushes. They were built on a slope, and behind them he saw cultivated ground that stretched quite a distance in terraces up the mountainside.

This is what he wanted to find. He placed his hand reassuringly on the Beretta. Then his phone buzzed. He was hoping it was Chris. He'd tell Chris to drive to the end of the road and wait for him. And stay on the line, should he find anything.

But it wasn't him; it was Katie.

"Where've you been?" she said in a high voice.

"Cambodia."

"What?"

"Back in the bush. More like the center of the island. We have a tip. We're looking for Doug Manley and Hank Crenshaw."

"Who are you with?"

"Chris. He's in a car. I'm on a trail."

"Did you hear about the remains and the identification?"

"No! What happened?" Sweat streaked down Standt's ribcage from his armpits. It dried in white salty streaks. He took a section of his shirt and wiped the sweat that dripped and stung his eyes.

Katie sighed, relieved. "It's not Amanda."

"Who is it?"

"Some local named Laney Jentess. They think it's murder, drugs related."

Standt stared at the house, trying to talk in hushed tones. He saw a man come out on one of the patios carrying a rifle. The man. heavy-set, shirtless, bearded, and tattooed, looked intently around the dense foliage. Standt walked to the edge of the trail and hunched down in the bushes. He still had the phone to his ear.

"Katie, wait…"

She was still talking on the other end. "They used dental records, not DNA."

"Katie, I'll call you back."

He watched the man, who scanned the area. The armed guard was then joined by a second, skinnier one; a shock of red hair and clutching what looked like an automatic pistol. Standt was on the trail about one hundred fifty yards away from the house, when he heard a loud engine and tires hitting the ruts of the road he had just walked away from.

# # #

Carla stood on the porch of her bungalow in Hanalei Town, smoking a cigarette. She scowled and blew out a cloud of stale smoke, which lingered in the torpid air and gave it a harsh, moldy scent. It was local pollution. She understood why no one wants to hang around smokers anymore, if they ever did.

Her cell phone lay on the railing to the porch. She took one more drag, exhaled and savored the left-over taste, before she stubbed the butt out by crushing it against the wooden railing.

She stared off into her backyard, which faced the mountains but was blocked by vine-strangled hardwoods.

She almost tossed the butt into the yard, but spotting an empty plastic glass of beer, gone warm and rancid in the sun, made her feel sloppy and thoughtless, so she put the butt down for a moment on the railing next to the cell phone.

She picked the phone up to call Detective Standt. He'd given her his card. She looked at it, then punched out the number. She felt the rise of agitation that commonly preceded snatching another smoke.

That guy she'd told Standt about, he seemed to know the scruffy woman who'd joined Amanda and him on the terrace. The one who brought the paper bag, filled with the unknown goods. The woman's name was Laney Jentess. Carla had seen her picture in the newspaper. Her remains were found on Hideaways the other day. Now Carla's Kauai world seemed to be falling apart.

The man probably killed the poor woman, who'd already looked the recipient of many hard knocks in life, and now something has happened to Amanda. Carla had to tell the detective, who would take action faster than the police. He seemed to be focused on Amanda's trail, more than anyone else.

He didn't answer the phone, then Carla listened to the short message. She looked up at the clouds settling on Waialeale like a black, foreboding blanket.

CHAPTER 31: TURNER ESPRAY

She had her sunglasses on and she looked out the aircraft window. She let her eyes linger on the Pacific Ocean. The sun made shadows of the clouds on the sea, which was empty except for frothy wavelets that broke along its surface.

She had two first-class seats. She sat in the one by the window. She kept the other one empty so no one would pry. So no one would tip off the paparazzi, or tell her how they idolized her, or even pretend not to know who she was, but in a conspicuous manner that was annoying and intrusive in its own way.

Her golden blond hair was tied back in a blue scarf. Brian Caleb, "Steam" they called him, was a personal bodyguard who sat reading a magazine across the aisle.

Amanda Wilcox was gone and she was flying out to Hawaii to lend a hand. She would do anything she could. She considered Amanda a dear friend in the friendless world of the famous. No expense would be spared.

She hadn't been able to get Amanda and her plight out of her mind. It wasn't just the awful tabloids and their salacious tastelessness. Absolutely nothing was sacred to them.

It was the ambiguity of "disappeared." The unknowns. Amanda had vanished into thin air. There was something impotent about the efforts to find her, a giving up on the case. It was in all the papers. She had to do something. She knew she had the power and the influence; what happened to her friend outright haunted her evenings.

She'd always looked up to Amanda, even when strangers grew to idolize Turner Espray.

She'd joined Amanda at one of the GMO protests, and the experience was exhilarating. Her presence had a potent effect on the media coverage and what people thought about food poisons. For once, she'd felt like she was making a difference, not just another movie.

The irony was rich, but Turner wanted to *be* like Amanda, even as her own status skyrocketed to the stars. She wanted people to accept her for her brains, not just for her beautiful body and sultry moods.

She had a magnetic sexuality that came across not only on the screen but in person. But it blocked out everything else she thought was important.

People listened to Amanda, were moved and inspired by her. People *watched* Turner; they wanted to glide like her. She had a certain eye-catching sway in her arms and hips. A life force that originated in her eyes and travelled down her curvaceous body.

There was that body. They wanted her beautiful olive eyes, her thick lips, and her large prominent breasts. They hung on the sound of her voice. She felt consumed.

She wanted to be taken seriously, but secretly knew that she wouldn't ever have the automatic respect people had for Amanda.

Actors and directors respected her, coveted her stardom. Even though other performers obsessed over that form of acceptance, it was almost becoming tiresome. Turner Espray felt like *Amanda* was the real thing. *She* was Amanda's friend and benefactor.

Turner couldn't yet hold a candle to Amanda's brand of modern femininity. She was jealous of Amanda's narrow activist fame, and imprisoned by her own actress' fame.

She was terrified of paparazzi and what they can do to your life. She thought of Princess Di. She ordered another tomato juice from the steward.

Amanda was just as good looking as she was in high school, but taller.

Turner knew men, all too well. She had her pick of them. She thought what had happened to Amanda had to do with a man. Or men.

She was going to spend the better part of a week on Kauai. She had some phone numbers, of an investigator and a reporter who were on the island. She was determined to get to the bottom of this calamity. She would want Amanda to do the same thing, if Turner disappeared.

She took off her glasses, and leaned her head back against the soft seat back. She closed her eyes. She wondered if anyone was staring at her.

# # #

Katie Hudson's name was right alongside Standt's on Turner's contact list. When she couldn't locate Standt, she called Hudson.

The reporter couldn't believe it. Normally assertive and confident in person and on the phone, she was struck dumb for what seemed an eternity, but it might have been ten seconds.

Not long after talking to Standt as he made his way through the jungle, Katie got another call that had a New York City area code.

The voice on the other end was calm, sultry, a little hoarse. Instead of saying "Is Katie Hudson there?" the caller paused a pregnant moment then said, "This is Turner Espray."

After the stunned pause, Katie just said "Yes!" a little too emphatically, eagerly. Her instincts told her this wasn't a mistake, a hoax. She knew who Turner was and had a passing familiarity with the actress' connection to the case.

Anyone who followed Amanda Wilcox knew that Turner Espray was in the middle of the episode.

It was like the famous people who line up for a cancer fundraiser. They sense their personal power. They want to do something good, and perhaps the guilt of celebrity, the knowledge that they receive far too much attention and adulation than they deserve, has something to do with it too.

"I'm in Kauai now, and I really want to help! God help Amanda, I want to do anything I can."

Turner said this with a voice that was sensuously low but carried real feeling.

"I write for *Slate*. I've been covering the story," Katie replied somewhat awkwardly. Espray partly interrupted her. She was used to nervous phone conversations, but she also conveyed warmth and caring. She wanted to settle Katie down and get on with the business of Amanda.

"Can you come to my villa?" she asked.

"Of course."

"It's in Kilauea. I'll send a car. When can you make it? Is an hour okay?"

Katie couldn't contain her excitement. "Yes, easily!" Her eyes darted around, looking for her iPad and notebook. She would need both. And her cell phone. She had Standt's car, but that would stay in the driveway. But what if Standt needed a ride?

She'd cross that bridge when she got to it.

"A dark-blue SUV will pull into your driveway, and it will be Steam," Turner chuckled, totally relaxed. "I'm going to give you his cell-phone number, and you can give him your exact address."

She was putting Katie at ease. "He looks like he might play college ball, but he's really a fine musician. You can't miss him. And oh one other thing, and this is really important."

"What?"

"Don't tell a soul I called you. Or that we're getting together. Or, where I am, God forbid."

"I wouldn't..."

"You won't believe the hell that would unleash..."

"I totally understand."

"Seriously, the paparazzi, the press...remember, we're doing this for Amanda. We don't need any distractions. I just really need to speak with you in person. I want to find out everything I can do. It's terrible...horrible...I think we can get to the bottom of it, though. You know, I knew Amanda in school."

"I know...I know how you feel."

Katie was excited to tell Standt about the actress. She wasn't exactly sure what effect Turner would have on the investigation, but they would use it in whichever way they could.

The Kauai authorities would probably cower at their feet if Turner Espray said they needed anything, like extra manpower. Then the Chamber of Commerce and tourist folks would turn the visit into a PR bonanza.

The SUV showed up in the driveway sooner than she thought it would. The driver, Brian Caleb, was nicely dressed in a white tennis shirt and well over six feet. He reminded Katie of Tiger Woods.

"Ready to go see Turner?" he said.

"You bet."

They mostly rode in silence, with Katie looking out the window and wondering where Standt was. It was weird that he hadn't returned her latest call. They were keeping tight communications throughout this trip.

"It's a beautiful island," Caleb said after they were out on the main highway toward Kilauea. "I sure hope we find something on Amanda Wilcox."

"Ever met her?"

"Yeah. A couple of times. I like her. She's one of those people who has their head screwed on straight, if you know what I mean. She wants to make the world better. Hard to find that nowadays."

"Does anybody at all know that Turner Espray is here?"

"Airline people. That's about it."

They pulled off the road on to a private drive that had a corridor of tall banyan and eucalyptus trees. The villa lay in the distance with the blue ocean and horizon behind it.

CHAPTER 32: TRAPPED

Standt stepped off the trail and into the underbrush as two men pushed a manacled Chris Ke' alohilani in front of them.

"What're you going to do?" Standt heard Chris say. He was sweating through his t-shirt and had his arms pulled back tightly behind him. He still wore sandals as he stumbled along with a grimace. One man pulled him from the front by his forearms. That man had a pistol in a holster strapped onto his left hip.

"Just clam up," the man in the lead said.

"What were you doing back here?" the man behind Chris asked him. Standt recognized him from pictures as Doug Manley. He had a sweaty, mangy-dog look about him. His lank brown hair fell into his eyes, and taut, tattooed arms sprouted from a shirt from which the sleeves had been scissored away.

"I wanted to see where that road went," Chris said.

"That's all."

"It seemed like you were looking for someone, or something. That right? You didn't see the No Trespassing signs? You broke the law, son. We don't allow that here. It don't look like we got the law here…" He rambled on drunkenly.

"Now I know the signs are there–you can let me go."

Standt took pictures with his cell phone when they were still too far away to hear the clicking of the device. Then he silently sent the pictures attached to empty text messages to Church and Katie.

He didn't have time to actually type a message or check any unanswered phone calls. He shoved the cell phone back in his pocket, crouched down farther as they got closer, and slowly removed the Beretta from his pocket. It felt cool, heavy, and firm in his right hand.

The people grew large through the spaces in the underbrush. Their feet scuffed along through the red dust; he could see Chris' bare feet and sandals. Standt's thighs were getting stiff from crouching down. Sweat dribbled down behind his sunglasses into his eyes. He swabbed at it with the back of the hand that held the handgun.

The men moved slowly down the trail in a shuffle. The air was thick and hot, the weeds barely moving. The first guy was the stout guard Standt had first seen. He had a thick beard and khaki pants. Beneath the camouflaged bush hat, he looked like the parody of a soldier of fortune.

Standt thought that he needed to disable the safety on the gun and free the extra ammunition. He put the gun down about three feet away under a bush and reached for the magazine when the leaves crunched behind him and he darted around, but not before a blunt object came down on the back of his head.

He went black and fell over and rolled halfway down

a hill through grasses and rocks. That only took seconds. Afterward, he was partly conscious, blinking and throbbing and trying to figure out what just happened. He had the sensation of laying on hard ground but not being able to move. Blood flowed down the back of his neck from where a man had struck him with a rifle butt.

\#   #   #

Standt was splay legged on the floor, his back against a wall. The room was cast in shadows with only a single chair for furnishings. The air was fetid and dusty and didn't move a breath; he could see light coming through slits in a shaded window.

He was in a sitting position, the scabbed bloody head leaning back on a plaster wall. The bleeding had stopped but his head glowed. It was tender where it rested against the wall. When he looked around, the scene was framed in a dark halo. Both his hands were bound at the wrists behind him.

The binding was hard plastic, as in zip ties. The room had the feel of a crude prison, bare cracked walls with stains on them, but he was alone. He knew what had happened, that he was in deep shit. The blow hadn't erased his memory. He wondered where Chris was.

He wondered whether Chris was dead, and if he was eventually going to be shot in the head and left somewhere deep in that jungle below the mountains, where his body would rot unfound.

Too many people knew where he was at the moment, but Manley and the other captor might simply be stupid and kill him anyways. They might have gotten used to killing people, so that the act didn't register with them. He'd met people like that, unalloyed psychos for whom murder has become banal. Killing is one of the things you do during the day, no more no less.

He could hear loud voices coming through the wall.

"What are we going to do with them?" one guy said. "Somebody's going to be looking. Then what?"

"I hid the Jeep," another said, in a low, sheepish voice.

"Now we can't let them go."

He heard a door slam and some footsteps.

When he touched the roof of his mouth his tongue stuck there. He blinked away sweat from his eyes, or maybe it was blood. He began to try to get up, using his legs for leverage as he pushed himself against the wall. The effort was too difficult and he slumped back down.

Then the door gave way and two men stood there. The sunlight was blinding and piercing when they opened the door. Standt thought they were the two he'd tried to snap pictures of, with Chris. He shut his eyes and opened them again on to the two looming, unkempt men. They stood in the middle of the floor and looked at him menacingly as if *he* had done something. The glare was accusatory.

"What the fuck are you guys doing? Let us go," Standt mumbled. His face, the muscles around his jaw, didn't seem to be working very well.

"Give him some water," Manley said.

The tall fat guy put a plastic bottle to Standt's mouth and upturned it. A lot of the water dribbled down his cheeks but he got some of it. The guy had a plastic bag in his other hand.

"You were creeping around our property, like you were going to steal stuff. I had to tie you up, keep you here. You seemed dangerous."

"We didn't even know you existed back here."

"Now you do. And that's unfortunate for you," Manley said. He pulled a pint flask out of the side pocket of his pants and took a greedy guzzle, until it was gone and he dropped the bottle on to the floor. It made a perfunctory thud and slid about a foot.

The hard booze didn't look like the kind of stuff you would ever want to drink in the heat, but maybe he was so out of his gourd that he was permanently numbed.

"I'm an NYPD officer and lots of people know I'm here."

Manley scoffed. "You're full of shit. You're in the bush now, pard. No one's finding you here."

"You can let us go, then you'll have plenty of time to get out of here." Standt shifted his legs and his back, trying to get more comfortable. "Where's the other guy?"

"Shut the fuck up. He's being taken care of."

The fat guy was setting up some kind of contraption in the far corner of the room, like a camp cooker. He was lighting a little fire.

"What's that?" Standt said, staring at it. He wondered if Church, or Katie, had gotten his pictures yet.

"Lunch," Manley mumbled.

"Let the other guy go. He just gave me a ride out here. He's mellow. He's a local surfer, a pothead. He won't say anything. He doesn't care about what goes on out here. He just stoned all the time."

Manley scoffed at that too. "I know Chris Ke' alohilani. He's a cop. Who're you tryin' to fool? You tryin' to lie to me? What do you think, I'm a moron? I can't count on his silence. You see, I have a problem. Two problems, actually. You…and him. I have to find a solution. You guys caused a lot of trouble by poking your puss into my business. What do you expect me to do? Let you go with a little pat on the ass?" He waved his veiny arms around. He was almost obscured in the red dust raised by his feet stamping around. The ochreous dirt seemed to have permeated everything. "What would *you* do?"

Standt thought for a moment. Manley was looking at him with a sneer. Lank greasy brown hair came down to his shoulders and he had a few days old red beard. His arms were tattooed and the skin and his t-shirt were dirty. He looked like he'd been doing physical labor in the bush, but Standt knew it was only because he'd been on the run.

Manley was waiting for an answer.

"Come clean and call your lawyer."

Manley laughed, almost good-naturedly. "You're an out-of-towner. What's your name anyways?"

"Karl Standt. I'm a well-known New York detective." He thought of Amanda in Manley's hands. He wondered if he'd stumbled upon what they were looking for…Amanda's captors. He wondered where her body was.

"They'll be a big stink if I vanish out here," Standt went on. "You can disappear–you know the territory. Just let us go. Make us walk out of here. We don't have a phone. That'll give you plenty of time to get off the island. Wherever. We'll not be able to go very fast in our condition.

"If you come clean and let us go now, they might not be able to get you for kidnapping."

Manley paused for a moment, staring at Standt vacantly. "Nice try. Are you a lawyer?"

The room had a stench of burnt oil. "What's that?" Standt said. "Be careful with that thing. You'll start a fire in this…dump."

"Don't worry about that," Manley said.

"It's the first course," the big guy said, over his shoulder. "You'll like the menu here…seafood…" Then he cackled idiotically.

"That's Big Dan," Manley said, as though Standt needed a formal introduction. "He does everything big. Eats big, looks big, drives a big car, carries a big gun. Has a big mouth."

"Likes big women…" Dan said, and they burst forth with vapid laughter.

A little flame heated a bowl, and Big Dan was sifting white powder from a small zip-locked bag into the bowl. This went on for about a minute.

Standt licked his desiccated lips.

"This is going to feel really good," Manley said. He was speaking with a whiny, disrespectful voice as though Standt was a little boy. "It's an *experience.* I've got to say, a *new* experience for you. And the best thing about it is, you're going to forget about everything you've seen and heard here."

Big Dan got out a hypodermic needle and syringe. He put the needle in the little bowl and began to draw up the melted substance. It was the color of black licorice mixed with milk.

"Don't do this," Standt said. "Don't you do that."

"You want me to kill ya instead?"

Standt's head was swimming, and he still tasted blood in his mouth.

He thought of junkies he'd seen in New York, hundreds of them over the years. The ones living in poverty and squalor, the human decay. Squatting in abandoned buildings with rags and urine stains in the corners. The needles discarded around the room, contaminated by HIV virus and hepatitis. It only took once.

The man came over with a rubber hose and seized Standt's arm. Standt ripped it back from him. "Don't do that!" He yanked his arm back from Big Dan's grasp, until finally the man punched him in the jaw and Standt cried out from the pain in the back of his head.

Now his jaw swelled, and the man tied the rubber hose tightly around his left biceps. Then he bent over and picked up the needle. "Don't fight it," he said. "You'll spill the goods…"

Standt broke out in a sweat that poured down his neck and the sides of his face. He began to squirm away from Dan.

"Oh no, look at the tough New York cop now," Big Dan taunted. "I thought you guys were primo, brazen. Now you're a scaredy-cat. Take away the swat team and the helicopters…"

"If you have to do this I'll snort it," Standt blurted out. Anything but the needle. He'd seen models who snorted, exclusively. They still became junkies, without the perforated arms and scabbed spaces between the toes. None of it was any kind of pretty–the snorting of the drug was the top alternative in a decadent world gone mad.

"I was afraid of shots too when I was a kid," Dan whined facetiously. Then he held the needle up to Standt's beefy shoulder muscle. Standt bellowed in rage and fear with a noise he didn't recognize. He saw the Kauai sunlight shining brilliantly over the dirty floor.

CHAPTER 33: DAMAGE

Hank Crenshaw was in the bungalow. It was located farther up the tangled hillside, and gave him a view of the dirty little hovel where Manley was keeping two prisoners.

They usually used that wooden structure, moldering in the torrential rains and beginning to come apart from neglect, to store plastic-wrapped and duct-taped packages of pot, hashish, heroin, and cardboard boxes of various pharmaceuticals, mostly painkillers. They easily sold that stuff on the black market.

Now he stood outside sipping a cup of coffee that contained chopped-up ice and two fingers of Jack Daniels.

Everything was beginning to come apart at the seams, not just that building. He'd heard the loud voices coming up from the lower house, now silence.

Manley was a psycho, and now he's taking the whole operation over the precipice. Crenshaw had heard that two plainclothes cops were imprisoned in the storehouse and were having drugs injected into them. Then what, were they just going to let them starve to death? Other cops, probably feds, would be looking for them. Four-wheel drive vehicles, SWATs, and choppers. Crenshaw was planning his escape for that week. It was the only way out.

Manley's turning the bunch of them into serial killers. Crenshaw once was in proximity to people who died, but it wasn't his fault. That kid who fell off the roof at Boston College was acting crazy and asking for it. But no one believed Hank. He was lucky he dodged that bullet, but now they had Laney's body to deal with.

It was discovered on the beach.

People are starting to put two and two together. Laney knew too much about the drug business for sure, but the next thing he knew was that Manley told him she was dead. That other psycho Big Dan probably did it. Those two don't know how to deal with things without killing. It's come to that.

Crenshaw finished the odd mixture of iced coffee and Jack. Then he saw the door open to the storehouse and Big Dan and Manley come out into the shadows and tall weeds and grasses. Black clouds had settled over the steep slopes, a massively dense and green rug of jungle that exhaled wisps of fog.

He couldn't believe he'd be leaving all those poppy plants and pot orchards behind. Millions of dollars worth of product, but Crenshaw was too hot to stay on Kauai. He couldn't even fly out of Lihue; he'll have to take a motor boat, in darkness, maybe to Nihau first. Because no one would expect him to go there.

He poured only Jack Daniels and ice into the glass now. He'll have one more. He has to have his head somewhat straight for the escape. Manley didn't even know Crenshaw was going. Manley had gotten to the point where he just killed people because they were getting in the way.

She's only doing this because she needs her Vicodin. The words repeated themselves in his mind like a scratchy record he couldn't stop.

Then Hank got Laney the dog-lady, all those dogs she kept in her bungalow, scroungy mutts, to supply Amanda with her pills.

They met her one day on a boat when she was paddleboarding. He took her in broad daylight, then Amanda became a junky. It was that simple. The heroin was a path to what he wanted, like those rutted, red dusty roads that men had gouged out of the jungle.

It now seemed like the stupidest thing he had ever done, all for a sick love he had felt for Amanda. One that would never be reciprocated. In fact, she had a contempt for him. It fairly dripped from her eyes.

He grimaced, drained the glass, and hurled it into the woods. Then he ducked back into the bungalow before Manley and Big Dan saw him.

CHAPTER 34: ACUTE COORDINATES

The photos from Standt were weird. Church knew exactly why. They showed bushes from a strange angle, with acutely angled sunlight singeing the lens. Two shadowy distant figures on a dirt path. They were taken awkwardly. The detective was no expressionist photographer.

Standt had successfully sent the hacker the geographical coordinates for his location.

All Church did was extract the latitude and longitude embedded in the images. The camera could connect with the GPS and put that geographical data into the photo. It was very accurate, to within several yards.

Amazing technology, and now most ordinary people know how to use it. Hell, you can go to a map online and position little pins where your pictures were taken.

It couldn't be easier, unlike hacking into Verizon and AT&T. That remained a black art.

Church leaned back in the airline seat and tried in

vain to stretch out his long skinny legs. He clawed at a nearly empty bag of Cheezits and mixed nuts that he'd stuffed into the seatback, then collapsed back into the awkward sitting position.

He not only had the ability to execute those hacking commands from a text prompt on his laptop, and thus enter the wild and wooly world of U.S. telecommunications. He could also put two and two together. The message: "help me a.w." made complete sense to him now.

The text originated from a geographic point in Kauai very close to where Standt had taken those photos.

It was only sent a few days ago. Good ole Standt. He's in the thick of it again. He's probably found Amanda Wilcox. Hope she's still alive. It's so weird. How did she get into the jungle in the first place?

Some asshole kidnapped her.

Church was sitting in the aisle seat as the aircraft circled an approach to Lihue. He was vegged out, with a narcotics hangover. He and iz had been hitting it a little heavy lately. He missed her already.

He had good information about Amanda at his fingertips. The thing is, what was he going to do *now*? It wasn't as if he could hail an airport cab and tell the driver, "Take me to latitude 41, longitude 55, where felons and psychos live in the jungle."

He'd get in touch with that chick Katie. She'd want to know where Standt is. She probably had money, an expense account, knew people. We'd get a vehicle and some other guys and get our asses out there.

CHAPTER 35: PARADISE LOST

The drug hit his brain like a tanker-truck. His face rocked forward and his head nodded. Then his whole body seemed to liquify. He melted into a prone position on the floor. His heartbeat got all rubbery and slow. All was good and serene. It was a guilty pleasure. He could sit in his own urine, and he wouldn't mind it.

He wasn't hot and dying of thirst. The floor was like soft sand. He didn't care anymore about Big Dan, who melted away like a benevolent nurse, carrying the works in his left hand.

A shade came down then it was all muffled voices and a deep dreamy sleep. He was on the New York subway with his mother and brother. Everyone else on the car was a mannequin. He didn't want to look at their plastic lifeless eyes, looking everywhere and nowhere at the same time–they were too unsettling.

His brother Joey, limping and bent over from his

injuries in Iraq, got up and walked into an adjoining car. He wanted to talk to somebody. "Be careful!" Luanne Standt cried out.

She was in her eighties but Karl looked into her face and the way her skin wrinkled and fell along her facial bones made her seem one hundred twenty. Yet her voice was still strong, still the voice of Ma.

"Between the cars! Watch out!"

They came up out of the subway and called a cab. The driver drove the wrong way against the traffic on the FDR drive. Huge tires had come loose from trucks and came rolling at them.

Standt made the driver pull over to let he and his mom out on First Avenue, from where he knew they could walk across town to his loft. But his missing brother left a deep chasm in his soul. It was the dream's obsession, which took him through several painful worlds.

Then he had the sensation of being moved. Someone on each arm. He pulled away, wanted to stay in the soft sand. Someone grunted, but Standt's own reply came out low and distorted. Minutes blended into hours and merged into days. He lived another lifetime.

Then a rawness settled in as the opiate wore off, a scalding light in his head. He was famished and thirsty. Pain came back with slow relentless throbs in different parts of his body. Blood trickled out of his nose, uncontrolled. A jaundiced light shone in his eyes.

He turned away and his tender cheek and nose nudged against the wall, and when he turned back and opened his eyes, he saw Amanda Wilcox.

# # #

Everyone was looking for Standt and Chris, including Bruno Reilly. They didn't give him a moment's peace. He was also trying to find Doug Manley, the loser.

The north shore of the island was suddenly a clusterfuck of crime; first Amanda Wilcox vanishes, then Manley's knife fight, then the brawl at the golf club.

Laney Jentess' torn-up remains washed up on Hideaways Beach, and now the island's politicos and investors and tycoons and chamber-of-commerce presidents were in an uproar. What was happening to our garden-island paradise? It was becoming more like Chicago or The Bronx.

People are going to stop coming to Kauai. Hawaii is supposed to be a tranquil escape.

Not only was Ted Rand in the process of cutting him off but he was just about to lose his sheriff job due to this crime wave.

It had something to do with this Detective Standt. He had a way of roiling the universe. All the while he thinks he's putting it back together. It all started when he arrived, at the time the Wilcox thing was blowing over, starting to lose steam.

Bruno rounded up every deputy and semi-deputy he could find, armed them, then they drove south in two SUVs to head into the bush. Bruno wanted to clean things up in Kauai. He thought he was back in the Dorchester section of Boston again, making a middle-of-the-night gang-banger arrest.

# # #

Amanda lay on a couch, staring at Standt. Then she put one arm on the armrest of the couch and pushed herself up into a sitting position.

Her eyes were sunken. Beneath the eyes the skin was a gray, fishy color, with tiny red capillaries wriggling across it. Her hair was long, greasy, and a darker brown. She was wearing clothes that didn't fit her; a short-sleeve shirt with four of the the buttons undone and the top of the garment tight across her broad shoulders. She had on a man's khaki shorts.

She had bare feet, and the nails were still painted beet red.

Her skin was too white for Kauai. Standt stared at a cluster of marks on the inside of her forearm. It looked like a rash on the whiter skin. She looked down and winced when she saw him looking at it.

"Who are you?" she said.

"Karl," he said, after a pause. "Are you Amanda?"

A long pause. "Yes," she said, breathing deeply, as if she had just rediscovered herself. Then her face failed and tensed up; a profound sadness drooped over it, as dramatic as a mime's.

She put her face in her hands and sobbed. Her shoulders shook with the sobs, then she looked up. The reddened eyes and the cheeks ran wet.

"Will you take me out of here? Can we go?" She began to stand up. Standt held an arm up.

"Wait," he said. Then he realized for the first time that he wasn't bound. He felt around the shoulder at the scab. He was hoping the injection had been part of a dream. It wasn't.

She watched him. "So they're doing it to you too?"

"How long has this been going on?"

"I don't know–a year?" She'd only been missing less than three weeks.

"What else have they been doing to you?" He felt like crap but he wanted everything. The whole story. The shit storm revealed.

"I don't know," she repeated. Amanda began to cry softly. Standt got up unsteadily and first went to the window. It was locked. He looked back at Amanda.

"Did they rape you?"

She shook her head, as if moving the memory pieces around so that they'd fall into the right places. Then she said, "Yes."

"Who?"

"I don't know. Hank was first."

"Crenshaw?"

"Yes," she finally said with certainty.

Standt went over to the door and he heard voices on the other side. They were approaching, pausing. Arguing about something.

He walked over to another door near where Amanda sat. He slowly turned the knob and it stuck, locked. He said quietly, "Who else?"

She looked up to a ceiling, and her face failed again, with that droopy mime's sadness. Standt's heart sank.

"Two…I don't know their names. Two I think!" she said angrily.

Then she made a concerted effort to recover her composure.

"It's actually been almost every other night. With Henry," she said with an almost eloquence, as though she'd had a rekindled fling with a lover. She was putting it that way to make the unpalatable palatable.

"He starts with shooting me up."

Standt winced and turned away. The world he once knew had gone all-over haywire, topsy-turvy, as monsters fell over each other to do vicious and venal things to the innocent.

So he had to take a piece of furniture to throw through the window. There was only one window and two locked doors. The view through the window was obscured by vines and broad leaves that encircled and enclosed the bungalow. It was as if Kauai had come alive by the roots and was trying to eat the house.

A sallow hot light made its way through the thick weeds.

Standt desperately needed real air and water.

"Have you been outside yet?" Standt said, testing a nearby chair for the one he was going to hurl through the window.

"No. I haven't left this room, this fold-out couch."

"Did they bind you, confine you?"

"They had a chain on my ankle. The first days. When they made me take the drugs."

"Christ. Jesus Christ."

Hank would be the first one he'd bring down, then Manley and Big Dan in line. A righteous vengeance bristled up through his own fatigue.

They heard a knock on the door and a voice said "Room service." The door burst open and it was Big Dan with a sawed-off shotgun. He pointed the blunt barrels at Standt.

"Somehow I knew you'd be frisky. Sit down."

"Where?"

Standt was looking at the leveled shotgun and the distance from his foot. He had to do something. Circumstances, very negative ones, had crowded in on him. Desperate times called for desperate measures, but Big Dan stood too far away.

"The chair, wise guy, and put your wrists together again."

Doug Manley came in behind Dan. He also carried a handgun. Standt sat down reluctantly.

All the possibilities announced themselves in his mind at once. If Church got the pictures, or Katie, they know where he is and have alerted someone. Maybe Chris told someone where he was going. Where *was* Chris?

What were they doing to him?

"Where's the first guy you snatched?"

"You mean surfer cop?"

"Yeah."

"He's in another rec room. Don't worry about him."

"He's local. You can't keep him forever."

"Says who?"

Big Dan was the very picture of a sneer. The sneer started on his face and seemed to encompass his whole bloated body. Standt had an overwhelming urge to commit violence on him. His absence would mean an evolutionary improvement for the species, which nonetheless had projected its deeply flawed nature of late.

"Says logic. He has friends, family, other cops. You guys aren't safe here. Kauai isn't that big. It isn't Mexico. They're going to come looking for *him*, at the very least."

Big Dan would fit right in with the Mexican drug cartels. They'd use him for muscle for a while, then do something like chop his head off and drop the rest of his body in the dried up Rio Grande.

Dan shook his head and moved to a corner of the room. He had his bag, the works, with him.

"You just let me be the judge of that. I'd work on not being the nosey type, if I were you. You got into some shit here you never should have."

Manley walked over to Standt, aiming his handgun. "Cover him for a sec," he said to Dan, then he moved the barrel of the gun from Standt's head and wrestled another binding on to the detective's thick wrists.

Standt was sitting on a wooden kitchen chair.

When Manley was finished, he moved over to Amanda's couch and sat down next to her.

She shivered, wrapped both of her arms around herself, and shrunk away from him into the corner of the couch. The dowdy couch itself looked like something you would reserve for a couple of old cats.

"You two stay away from me," Amanda said, tearing up. The horror of her confinement and abuse had given her a self-protective, childish tone.

Standt wore a grimace of profound distaste and awfulness. Rage bubbled up and simmered.

"What's your problem?" Manley asked him, then laughed. "Let me guess, you don't approve. Of anything. But let me tell you this, I won't touch her. Hank won't let me. That wasn't part of our deal."

Then he looked at Amanda, as you'd offhandedly notice someone on a city bus.

"I wouldn't want to touch her anyways."

"You should let her go and get her to a hospital," Standt said.

Manley shrugged. "She's Hank's problem. He started it. The jilted boyfriend. Tch-tch. I'm busy, got a business going up here. Hank shows up one day with her. He's paying me rent and expenses. For services rendered.

"I agree with you," he went on. "It's a fucked up situation. It's a fucked up world. Isn't it Dan?"

"You said it," echoed the moronic oaf.

"She's got no future here," Manley said, staring at Standt. "She's not my responsibility. Take that up with Crenshaw."

Then he looked at Dan, who was bent over getting a needle ready. "What's taking you?"

"Fuck you. Think I like doing this? Feel like a fuckin' wet nurse." Then he walked over to Standt with the needle in his right hand.

"What's the purpose of this?" Standt said, his lips quivering and turning blue. He didn't know why that was happening. He wasn't scared; he was enraged. This room was

Hell's precipice, and he was going to take Big Dan and Manley to Valhalla with him. He vowed it.

Dan came forward with the needle and Standt thrashed around trying to free himself from the chair. "Hit him with the gun," Dan said to Manley. Standt stopped moving around. He could hear Amanda start to sob.

# # #

It was night. Light played around the edges of the darkness. Standt's head nodded forward, back and forward again, like a solemn rite. He was still bound to the chair. Slobber dribbled down his chin. Then his head fell forward and lolled there and didn't move back again.

He snored loose bloody goo through his nostrils.

Hours went by, days and weeks. It seemed years, a generation. They were hitting him up in the triceps muscle. Once, he opened his eyes and saw a bandage there, hiding a couple of dots. He didn't know whether he'd eaten, neither could he compute the passage of time.

His vision was crammed with misshapen faces, as if Salvador Dali and Willem de Kooning had been poured all at once into his skull. He felt like his own face had become one of those faces, with his cheeks too prominent and his chin hanging down somewhere near his ankles.

He opened his eyes and looked up. He knew he was still in a room with Amanda, as if by some miracle. She was a dark lump over by the couch sleeping.

Then someone poured cold water on his head. He was shocked, then he desperately tried to lap it up as it ran past his lips. "Some…" he gurgled.

"Okay okay," the man answered. Then a bottle came to his lips, turned upward, and he guzzled what he could. The bottle came down.

"This is your lucky day," Hank Crenshaw whispered.

He had a kitchen knife in his hand. He began to saw at the plastic bindings.

"We gotta move fast," he said. "I'm doing you a big favor." It seemed like the middle of the night. Standt could see Amanda stir in the dark. She got part of the way up.

"Who is it?" she said.

"Hank." Crenshaw watched her for a sign of familiarity but she was silent. That was hugely and delusively arrogant, Standt thought, to think that she would have an iota of feelings for him.

Standt looked out the window, through a broken, partially lowered shade. Moonlight shown somewhere behind the suffocating vines and leaves.

"Did you even give her a shower?" he asked Crenshaw, as the man worked on the binding behind him.

"Yes."

"How often?"

"What difference does it make? I'm letting you go." Everything about his entrapment there made Standt sick to his stomach.

Then the confinement in his arms fell free. But the blood flow had been cut off from them, so they tingled and flopped around uselessly.

"You get out of here, before the two monkeys wake up. And bring her with you. It's dark, they won't see you. Just take the trail."

Standt could see Amanda get up slowly, stand, and hold on tentatively to the edge of the couch. Crenshaw was just standing in the dark, looking at Amanda, then he grunted and walked over to the door. Standt heard the door squeak.

This was all for Crenshaw's sake, his fragile conscience. "Hurry up!" Crenshaw whispered.

CHAPTER 36: DIGITAL BREADCRUMBS

Church had a few things on the people Standt were looking for. Doug Manley and Hank Crenshaw. Suffice it to say, they had no redeeming features.

It was odd and a little alarming that they hadn't found Standt yet. He hadn't called either one of their cell phones, or texted, or emailed. Time to follow his GPS tracks, the digital breadcrumbs.

The giant hacker stood outside the small Lihue Airport terminal, holding on to his single canvas bag. In it, he had stored an XL tied-dyed t-shirt, and extra briefs, for the times when he actually wore underwear. That was it for extra clothes, the rest of it was his laptop and cell phone.

Katie was picking him up. He'd emailed and texted her and she answered right away.

He'd met her with Standt at a restaurant once

downtown. She was a hot chick, a writer in the city. That was pretty cool. She was nervous now. He didn't blame her; he was worried about Standt. And he'd never been worried about Standt before.

Kauai must be like the endless holiday, he thought, waiting for her car. The chickens are weird, as in, no one's looking after them or doing anything. They run wild through the airport. Then Katie's Honda rental car pulled up.

Katie recognized him right away, a six-foot-nine guy with long platinum colored hair and studs in his ears. He was impossible to miss. She didn't say anything when he squeezed into the backseat, and attempted to stretch his elongated legs out.

Then she was back out onto the highway and heading north towards Princeville.

"You said something about the pictures," Katie said, brushing away the hair that was blowing into her face through an open window.

"I need wifi. I have the GPS coordinates, the exact ones. I need to put them on Google Earth."

It was a good thing Standt hadn't disabled geotagging on his phone. Or he'd be lost on Kauai for sure.

"Okay, I'll look for a coffee shop or something." It was only gas stations and coffee-bean plantations and bungalow neighborhoods by the side of the road. The traffic was bad. Katie was in a panic. She was gunning the accelerator and trying to pass people without a specific destination.

"So we find him on Google Earth, then what?"

"We drive there." Church dug his laptop out of his backpack.

"No. We can't do that. That's not good enough. I would have heard from him by now. Something's wrong…" Then the first thing that popped into her head was Turner

Espray.

The collection of buildings and trees they were passing was nearby her villa. At least, within about ten miles. She suddenly screeched on her brakes and jerked the car into the breakdown lane.

"What are you doing?" Church yelled out.

"I'm making a call!" She furiously dug into her cloth bag that was sitting on the passenger seat and found Espray's number.

The actress was anxious to help, do anything. Now they needed her.

CHAPTER 37: PURSUED

Standt had Amanda by the arm. Crenshaw moved ahead of them in the dark. They were still in the house. It seemed haunted by the presence of Manley, Big Dan, hypodermic needles, and the awful viscous solution those needles had dispensed.

The air was malodorous, hinting of decay. Their footsteps creaked along the floor. Standt could feel Amanda shivering along the long slim arm he held. She whimpered quietly.

"Shut up!" Crenshaw hissed. They came to a door. There was a stirring and shuffling behind a closed door down the hallway beyond. A grunt. Crenshaw turned quickly and put an index finger to his lips. Who knows. Maybe he was afraid of Big Dan coming out into the hallway and indiscriminately deploying that sawed-off shotgun. He'd probably seen him do it before.

They scampered down a rug-covered flight of stairs.

Standt's heart beat like a bird's. He had a thin layer of sweat covering his body. It was fear, narcotics withdrawal, or both. He'd worry later about what they had done to him and Amanda; the residual effects. Now they had a chance to escape. They were so close.

They came to a screen door. Crenshaw reached down, turned the knob slowly, and opened the door. He took one look back, whispered, "You're on your own."

Standt thought of Chris. He had to get Amanda out first. He'd come back for K.

He pulled Amanda closer to him as they eased through the doorway.

"If you can just get through this next hour, you'll be safe. It's freedom." She was close to collapse, hurrying through the door unsteadily with Standt at her elbow. Who could blame her, given the torture she'd undergone?

Standt gripped her by the bare upper arm and mostly held her up as they slipped through the screen door and out onto a weedy, unkempt, and neglected patch of beaten-down lawn.

The door swung back and cracked against its frame. He didn't have a free hand to stop it.

"Dammit. C'mon!" he whispered, hoping she could move her legs faster. He was half carrying her.

Ahead of them, Crenshaw snatched a small pack off the ground. He looked back once, then vanished into the night. The captor and torturer had become a temporary savior. It was the way things worked in the world Standt was accustomed to, a morally ambiguous realm in need of light and absolution.

Amanda sobbed louder, in relief. The moldering bungalow sat leaning into the jungle dark. It was now behind her. She fell down onto the soft ground. Standt picked her up and they scrambled into a space that opened in the underbrush. Trees bent over them in the darkness. There was only one place to go.

He looked back into the wall of trees and choking vines that shielded the house, for a sign of Manley or Big Dan. Nothing.

"Where are we going?" Amanda cried. "I want to stop. I want to rest!"

"We can't. We can't!" Standt said. The air was clear, and when he looked up the stars twinkled in the unblemished sky.

# # #

They scurried along the trail, each footfall in the thick leaves seeming to loudly broadcast their position. The next time Standt looked back, he saw floodlights on in the bungalow, a piercing light through the ferns and densely tangled tree trunks.

Light beams refracted through a vaporous fog of rot exhaled from the jungle floor. He urged Amanda on; she was in a weakened state that engulfed her body like a fever. It seemed like she weighed no more than one hundred pounds.

"Let go of me!" she said. This one conveyed vim and vigor. She seemed to be getting a second wind. "Where are you taking me?"

"To the road," he said. "You're going to have to trust me, Amanda."

"How do you know my name?"

"Everyone knows you," he said, then corrected himself. "Your father sent me, Sam Wilcox." The name of her dad brought a look of recognition and sadness to her face. She finally looked at Standt as more than just another man handling her roughly.

Standt halted for a moment. They were both breathing heavily, audibly. They made eye contact.

"He loves you. He wants you back. Safe and sound. You're his baby girl. Trust me."

Her hair was matted from neglect and the full-body sweats of narcotics cravings, but in the shade of the moonlit foliage he could detect a rekindled gleam in her eyes.

The life force was coming back. Tears replaced the gelid bleakness he'd seen in her eyes in the bungalow.

"I want to go home!" she gasped.

"You'll get there," Standt said. In the back of his mind, he doubted he'd survive the journey himself.

If Big Dan and Manley caught them he'd be killed; probably Amanda too. Their bodies would be flung off a cliff into the rocks and the sea, never to be found by people. That nature of endgame seemed all but inevitable.

As they scrambled down the trail he thought he saw shadows in the floodlights through the weeds; but he could hear no voices.

He vaguely recalled the trail as the one where he'd been clobbered on the head. Then he remembered the Beretta handgun. He'd placed it on the ground before he was hit. It was loaded, with the safety off. He watched the side of the trail until he came to the upturned part of it where he'd previously crouched down and watched Chris K. dragged along as a prisoner.

It was his last chance. He couldn't move Amanda fast enough to keep ahead. He felt amidst the moist leaves and rotting vegetation in the dark. He got down on his hands and knees, until he touched the Beretta laying in the dirt.

He picked it up in his right hand. It was reassuring, heavy. He felt a kind of joy as though the playing field had been leveled, by a small margin. "Got it," he said more to himself.

Amanda stood in the middle of the trail shivering. "Give me that gun!" she barked. The ferocity surprised him.

He hesitated then said: "If I'm dead you can take it from there. Get in here and wait."

She crept into the weeds and bushes beside the trail. The woods around them were partially lit up by the floodlights from the bungalow in the distance.

"You'll have to hide here. Don't say a word. Not a sound," he whispered. "You have to do this for me Amanda."

"What are you doing?"

Standt looked at the Beretta for a moment. He was too exhausted to mince words. He thought of Big Dan and Manley putting poison in needles then injecting them with it.

"I'm going to kill one or two men."

"Do it," Amanda said. She was breathing hard and staring at him.

"When the dust settles, when it's quiet, if I don't come get you in a few minutes, start moving. Go back down this trail until you find someone. Someone will be on the road. Eventually. You'll be free."

"What about you?" she said more plaintively.

"Don't worry about me. Just sit tight. Don't worry."

Standt thought of the fathers of the world, and their lifelong protectiveness toward their daughters. The thread that ties men together. The fatally flawed, malevolent world and its predators and the innocent women and children. He wanted to eradicate all of them–rid the world of its pestilence–beginning with men like Big Dan and Hank.

He felt like the world was watching him. Virtually anyone who read newspapers or watched cable had wanted Amanda back. Now she was in his hands.

# # #

Standt waited farther down the trail in the bushes. He lay on the moist earth on his stomach propped up on one elbow, with the handgun laying on the ground in his other hand.

The lights pierced through the jungle but no one came down the trail. He couldn't hear anything from Amanda. Good. He was afraid that, in the throes of withdrawal, she would cry or moan, and draw the gunmen towards them.

Now it was just the wind, the big banana leaves rubbing together, frog and cicada noises down below. His own heart thumping against the ground.

His eyes went down about halfway.

He wondered what his son Tim was doing right now. Twelve years old. Today was…he couldn't say what day it was. He had no sense of time. He didn't know how long they had injected the drugs into him. It could have been 36 hours; or 36 days. The drug is strange in its effects; it bent time. He couldn't say it involved pain; it was about control. And contaminating his bloodstream.

If he got out of here okay, he would get tested right off.

Maybe Tim was at school. Maybe they were singing, or working on computers; he could be outside and laughing in the sun in Central Park. Playing catch with a friend. He loved Tim. I love you Tim. Don't forget me Tim. Forget me not. Love me a lot. Then his head fell forward and the trickling water and wind through the trees became part of a dream.

The sun came up through the trees. He opened his eyes, to the flat, dirty, leafy ground. The side of his face had wet dirt and vegetative matter on it. He heard crickets; feet moving. A shuffling and voices. The light around him was crepuscular. He was still on his stomach lying in the bushes and he saw or heard no sign of Amanda.

Big Dan was in front with Manley, and two other

men, both carrying weapons, came up the trail behind them. Big Dan had a large flashlight and he was shining it into the bushes, strafing the area back and forth. Then he trained it on something in the bushes about ten yards from Standt.

"Now now. What do we have here?"

"Get away from me!" It was Amanda. Her legs poked through the weeds and bushes. Standt heard a desperate scrambling in the underbrush, like a frightened animal's.

Big Dan made a move toward the bushes beside the trail, but Standt stood up nearby in the shadows. The tropical sun came up fully, with dramatic orange light streaking across the horizon behind him.

"Get away from her. Drop the weapons."

Big Dan looked up. Three other men looked Standt's way. They had hooded eyes and slack smiles. Standt knew with the four of them, and his position given away, that this would be the briefest of conversations. Two men remarking on each other's presences.

Dan responded with a grunt. "You again."

Two simple words that a man utters, yet he never realizes that they are his last ones. The thoughts that cross-over his brain as electric impulses and manifest as spoken words are shut off forever.

NYPD detectives are trained to use their weapons only in life-threatening emergencies, and some go an entire career without discharging a handgun. Standt had once shot a murderer in the depths of the Manhattan subway tunnels. He'd knocked down another in a murky alleyway whose sin it was to have kept three dismembered victims in a basement freezer. It had taken Standt more than twenty-five years to end those two lives, but it was with no hesitation that he sent a slug crashing through the front of Big Dan's skull, then emptied the Berreta's nine-milliliter clip at the three other men, who also opened fire amidst Amanda Wilcox's lusty screams.

CHAPTER 38: THE FALLING

The helicopter's whirling blades parted the trees like a violent wind over soft grasses. Abner Vereen was back in charge, and in Cambodia.

It seemed like the real thing. The orange sun exploded over the mountains, jungle, and sea. Southeast Asia, he'd seen it once. And now he was using his helicopter as a pursuit aircraft again. All those vivid memories of combat over Iraq, of fear and pot and boredom and mayhem, came rushing back.

Two chicks and a tall hombre were in the backseat, Chris Ke' alohilani in the front. He was nursing a bruised face and body. Turner Espray was in the backseat.

He couldn't believe it. Katie called him last night and said they had ten thousand bucks to spend on the helicopter, then they showed up with Espray and her buff bodyguard, a dude they nicknamed Steam. He had an automatic rifle with him, and it was permitted. Abner made sure of that. He also knew where they were going was probably hot, and he got that old impending feeling of combat again, an admixture of fear and supreme, adrenal dread.

They didn't have room for the super-tall guy in his Goth get-up and platinum hair. The hacker. He seemed to know what he was doing on the technical side; he gave Vereen a collection of coordinates to home in on, even though the chopper didn't yet have GPS. That didn't matter; Abner knew where he was going, as they'd flown over the same spot just a few days ago.

Amanda might still be alive, and the detective was down there somewhere with her.

Of all the times Vereen should have been high for a helicopter ride, this was it. He was fueled only by adrenaline and caffeine.

They'd seen Chris K scuttling along near a narrow trail and landed the helicopter in a nearby open field. Chris had been beaten and held against his will. He was more angry than hurt. He'd escaped when the gang went looking for the fleeing Amanda and Standt.

Chris pointed the others in the direction up the trail, and they'd made two passes over a couple of partially hidden bungalows. It was a big plantation of poppies and marijuana or hashish was planted in bushes behind the decrepit building. But it didn't seem like anyone was inside the bungalows. They would have come out in response to the roar of the chopper just overhead.

Steam was crushed into the seat behind Abner. The strapping fellow had his automatic weapon pointed out the chopper at the jungle, like a Special Forces officer. Chris had filled them all in on the predation that had taken place in the bungalow, with Amanda Wilcox kept as a drugged prisoner. Vereen and all his passengers were elated she could still be alive.

This chick Espray was livid and *intensely* emotional about finding Amanda. Katie was beside herself. They were like two avenging angels. They were worked up to the point where Abner was almost feeling sorry for the perps, who were probably going to get castrated when these two powerful women caught them.

Then there was that detective; he was probably down there with Wilcox. He seemed like a survivor. The type.

Abner flew the helicopter along the tops of the trees, then Chris yelled at him that the bad guys were armed. Abner pulled the chopper back up to about two thousand feet, so they could scan the entire area. That's when they saw the man scrambling along a narrow trail on the edge of the steepest part of the mountainside.

The pilot looked over at Chris and the surfer nodded. Abner brought the helicopter down and buzzed the man, and Chris looked over at the two women. "It's Hank Crenshaw! I know it!" Chris had already briefed them. That Crenshaw was the prison warden and one of the rapists. He was the lead instigator.

They flew over Crenshaw again and he was standing on the trail looking up at them, shielding his eyes. He had a backpack with him, from which he pulled a handgun. Then he turned and ran up the rocky path. Katie screamed from the backseat, "Don't let him get away!"

Turner Espray gripped the back of Vereen's seat and yelled something like instructions to Steam. Steam aimed his weapon into the jungle near the man's footpath and suddenly fired into it.

"Jesus Christ!" The loud report startled Abner.

Crenshaw returned the fire. Chris could see the little puffs of cordite. He emptied his clip at them with rapid pops. The chopper veered away from the mountainside, with Steam firing back, this time right at Crenshaw, who ran along the trail with the gun at his side. Katie snapped pictures outside of her window the whole time. Abner arched them away toward the sea, and now he had a moderate impression of what life was like for an earlier generation of helicopter pilots, the ones in Vietnam. It's a sick feeling to have people aiming at you from below.

Steam's weapon was loud and it emitted a hot, oily black smoke and odor that trailed out the helicopter window.

"Don't lose him!" Espray yelled. Abner was thinking oddly, was this scene ever going to be covered by CNN? *Turner Espray and the helicopter assault.*

If they could pay ten grand for the story, he'd give it to them…if only they had some video…

He completed a circle, high above Kauai, with the steep, green, mountainside laying beneath them.

"Get him!" Katie yelled. "Then we'll go find Amanda! Don't lose 'im!"

"Hold your horses!" Vereen screamed back, with a grin so wide they could see all of his uneven teeth, mostly yellowed from the daily menthols. *Yeah, this was like the old days–the absolute crazy adrenaline of a firefight in the sky…*

He swung the chopper back to the mountainside and finally they picked out Crenshaw again. He was moving along the narrow trail like a tiny insect through its leafy habitat.

"Where does he think *he's* going?" Turner yelled out. Abner took a quick look into the backseat. Espray was wearing a red satin scarf, and had deep rouge on her lips. The helicopter carried her charisma, like an extra passenger.

Then he looked at Steam.

"You ready?" Abner said.

Steam nodded. "Yup." Then he bent over and tapped another magazine into his rifle.

Two pops came from below. Crenshaw just wouldn't give up. Steam fired a burst and Hank hit the trail, then scrambled back onto his feet, still gripping the gun. They could see the bullets strike the hard red earth, and between the rotor blades and the weapon, the sound was deafening.

Katie could see his face in the camera lens. The helicopter rocketed closer to him. His sweaty and dirt-streaked expression got all bunched up in anger and vengeance. Snap. The portrait squared off and leapt as a completed image into the corner of her LED screen.

He wore a massive sneer and he was yelling epithets at them, waving the gun in the air. Katie tried to picture him shooting Amanda up, then raping her. Here was the monster, down below.

Crenshaw was surrounded by steep red slopes marked by black volcanic rocks and clumps of vegetation.

She tried to hold the camera steady, as the helicopter bucked around. Then his eyes went wide; he disappeared from view. His right foot slipped and he tumbled off the trail. The helicopter veered toward the mountainside, then lurched away.

Katie looked back over her left shoulder. She saw Crenshaw claw at the mountainside. Then the body struck a rock and the arms and legs pinwheeled, hitting other stones and the cliffside with bursts of red and brown dust. At the end, his body was airborne, flailing out over blue waves crashing into giant, arrow-shaped pinnacles jutting out of Kauai's coastline. Crenshaw disappeared into the roiling seas.

The interior of the helicopter had only the loud engine noise. Everyone looked out their windows. Abner flew over the spot where they had last seen Crenshaw and they saw his body face-down and washed back and forth in the frothy waters. He was shark food now.

CHAPTER 39: RISING FROM THE ASHES

The rich red blood flowed down his leg from the shotgun pellet wounds. They'd smashed into him just above the knee. One had nicked his femoral artery. The blood pumped out and spattered on to the end of his shoe.

Now it was Amanda dragging *him* to his feet. The four other men lay on the ground; two were moaning and groping around for their scattered weapons. Big Dan was dead, as was one of the dog soldiers in the rear.

Manley was still alive.

Standt had lurched to his left while he was still emptying his clip at the four men, and this quick reaction had prevented the spray of bullets from hitting his head or upper body.

Amanda pulled him to his feet beside the trail. He handed her the gun, then ripped his t-shirt off to make a tourniquet. He could feel the juice going out of his brain as the blood pumped out. If he passed out, Manley would finish both him and Amanda off.

He pulled the makeshift tourniquet around his thigh above the widening, moistening wound as tight as he could. The sun blazed on the dusty, bloody tableau of still and crawling men.

"Where the fuck do you think you're going?" Manley grumbled, as he struggled to get to his feet.

"Home," Amanda said, defiantly, then she flashed a look at Standt. She had the Beretta in her right hand. He nodded. His mind was mush, but he vaguely recalled firing eight not ten shots.

"Get up close to him," Standt said.

Manley had a big beefy arm stretched out to grasp a sawed-off shotgun that lay on the ground next to Big Dan. Wisps of acrid cordite drifted along the moist ground.

Amanda took two steps with the barrel in both of her hands and perfunctorily, without ceremony, shot Manley in the head, as though putting an animal out of its misery, when in reality she was relieving some of the world's.

Standt said: "Let's get out of here."

He thought maybe they could out-pace the other wounded guy, who was lying on the ground holding his side, but didn't yet seem able to reach a loaded weapon. Amanda helped Standt to his feet and literally the walking wounded, they made their way down the trail.

Standt got weaker and weaker. Something was pulling a curtain down over his brain. The worst part of the bleeding was over, but the damage had been done.

"You go," he said to Amanda. "Watch the sky. Find the road. Just leave me. I'll be alright here." The words weren't coming out right.

"No," she said. Her certainty was back. It was as if

the old Amanda had returned. She'd sloughed off like a soiled, useless skin the one who was abused by needles and men.

"We'll make it together," she said. He was only on one leg, tied up with the red-soaked tourniquet, and she had the arm on his bad side. But he was a heavy burden. He collapsed roughly by the side of the road.

When he looked up the clouds scudded across the sky. The foliage was draped above him like a cathedral ceiling. The sun cast benevolent rays and he heard only the wind.

He felt a detached serenity and deliverance. It was an odd, twisted gratification, to die there of a gunshot wound by the side of the road. But the world had wanted Amanda back, and he'd found her. He'd done the grunt work and got her most of the way home. That was his deliverance. "Tell Tim…" he mumbled to Amanda, who stood above him, still holding on to his arm, talking in beseeching tones.

"You have to get up. We have to keep moving. I know you can do it!"

Darkness came over him like black ash drifting down from Kauai's sky. Hawaii's volcanos, blocking out the sun. It wasn't like sleep. He fought against it. In the background he heard:

"Don't do this Standt. Don't! You can make it! Don't do this to me!" The voice was high and girlish and had conviction. His eyes fluttered as he tried to jerk his brain back into that world, the one surrounding him as he lay in the red dust beside the trail, now stained with his darker arterial blood.

He saw Amanda looking down on him with a halo of tunnel vision around her head. Then he heard scuffling and heavy steps and voices. It couldn't be Manley's and Dan's people again. It couldn't. But he saw a big guy enter the circumscribed world of the dusty trail stained with Standt's blood and he recognized the flushed face and thinning, scraggly hair. It was Bruno Reilly and his posse of men.

Reilly came up and spoke gruffly: "Who are you?"

She looked up at him.

"I am Amanda Wilcox."

# # #

The helicopter descended like a metallic angel. They had Standt wrapped in an improvised litter. Bruno had an emergency kit. They'd been able to apply a tighter bandage to the wounds, and even gave Standt shots of morphine and adrenaline.

Kauai had a medevac service, but Abner was faster. He was already here.

For once in the past thirty minutes, Standt didn't think he was going to die. Fate had seemed to drift back over to his side.

He lay back in the sheet with both hands across his chest, like a statuesque apostle. Then Brian Caleb on the back and Bruno Reilly in the front, brought him over to the entrance to the helicopter.

The chopper's rotor blades made a metallic slicing noise as they severed the air about once per three seconds. Standt looked to the side and could see the gonzo pilot Vereen through the glass cockpit.

Standt had a half smile on his face as they deposited him in the back of the aircraft. It was good to be alive. He wondered how many lives he had left after cheating death once again; it couldn't be too many. He seemed to have marched through his adult life with a target on his back, which made the sun rising on the next day all the sweeter.

Where was Katie? She was walking beside him. Not far away was Amanda Wilcox with a blanket draped around her shoulders, next to her friend Turner Espray, who had her arm around the abused and plundered woman. The famous Amanda Wilcox, whom someone had tried to make a junkie out of.

Standt wondered whether Sam Wilcox was back in Kauai. Sam owed Standt a lot of money. What an invoice *that* would be.

He wondered what the world owed him, the undifferentiated millions who watched and read the news and wanted Amanda back in the worst way. Like lots of officers and detectives before him, that was an ongoing debt that was still piling up and would probably never be paid off.

Pain came back to his leg and throbbed up through his torso; he put his head back and closed his eyes, until it was gone. Steam and Bruno Reilly were crouching next to him; they better get him to some real medical personnel, and fast. He vaguely thought of shoving Bruno's face into the linoleum at the Princeville Golf Club, and the weird way that things come around on you.

The helicopter lifted off, on its way to Lihue Airport, from where he would be airlifted to a hospital in Honolulu. He could see the faces below watching them as the helicopter paused in mid-air, as though it was making its own decisions.

Then Vereen put them on a course for the hospital on the East Shore of the island. Before he shut his eyes, Standt watched the mountainside recede in the window, with the dark unwelcoming slope covered with an immense tangle of impenetrable jungle.

CHAPTER 40: THE HEALING

The vermin, Hank Crenshaw, Doug Manley, and Big Dan, were all dead. Standt found out about that soon enough. No one was going to bring them back, but unfortunately, the world that Standt knew kept recreating new versions.

Standt had been back in New York for a couple of weeks. He was walking with a cane. He was lucky that the pellets hadn't struck and decimated his knee, so that the knee didn't have to be replaced, for now. He *was* pushing fifty-three, so that might come later. He was also fortunate that there had been no infection or gangrene spreading from the gunshot wounds.

He kept going back to the doctors, and the nurses kept cleaning out the stitched up but still puffy and grotesque-looking wounds. At least the slugs were gone now, dug out by the original doctors in Hawaii.

Katie was back from Kauai, going through a kind of mental repair period of her own due to the trauma everyone experienced. It was a wild ride for her, especially in the end inside the helicopter.

She had thought Standt was going to die. She had actually gotten to know the benefactor of worthy causes, Turner Espray. Now Katie had written not one but a series of compelling articles on the Wilcox affair for *Slate.*

The photographs for that feature, especially the ones from the helicopter, of the bodies on the ground during a fly-over after Standt's shoot-out, and of Manley's vengeful face, were unforgettable. She was going to win some journalism award for them.

But what was most important to her was that she had gotten Standt back.

They had chatted about returning to Hawaii someday. Maybe they'd start in Maui. It would be unfair to perpetually condemn the islands because of what had happened there. They'd need a respite from the tropics first, however, let all the black memories and dark mojo blow over.

The big thing for Standt was waiting for the results of his HIV and hepatitis tests, given all of his exposure to the needles, and Big Dan's essentially unsanitary approach to the world.

Don Latham wanted a complete debriefing on the Amanda Wilcox story. Standt agreed to meet him for breakfast at the Plaza Diner on Second Avenue and 56th Street.

He'd decided to wander up Third Avenue from downtown, because it was such a nice day. He took his time, but that wasn't up to him. He had a cane, and a very large hole in his left leg, which was essentially made up of many smaller holes combining into one. It was a not-too-humid, sunny July day in Manhattan.

Sometimes his head fell back to gaze over the rooftops, and let the warm, but not scalding sunlight caress his face. Since having men try to kill him with sawed-off shotguns, he had more appreciation for his life's simple pleasures, as in the varied and delightful city walks.

Eased in amongst the martial-arts dens and the innumerable restaurants on side streets, he would pass outfits that offered tanning booths. People paid good money to lay down in a sort of pod and fry their pink skin with UVB rays, because they didn't want to pay for a plane ticket to places like Kauai. Standt shook his head. It seemed warped from his recent perspective. The wild world and the things people do.

The act of tanning made him think of the whole scene that had almost killed him down around the Tropic of Cancer.

He kept going until he found Latham waiting for him in a booth in the diner. He could see him through the window, drumming his fingers on the formica table. Standt figured that his lateness had caused an aggravation, because Latham couldn't smoke inside the restaurant and was trapped in the diner waiting for Standt.

Like the Madison Restaurant downtown a few blocks, the Plaza Diner was run by affable and hard-working Hispanic men. They never seemed to have a harsh word or foul mood. Eating in the diner made Standt feel grateful to be be in Manhattan again. Grateful to be alive.

"So this whole thing winds up to be due to one sicko," Latham said. Standt waved over one of the waiters and ordered a coffee and burger.

"Ultimately, yes. But he got tied up with a couple of other sickos. A whole motley crew of them."

Latham flipped open a small notebook. He was another traditional newspaperman who couldn't go completely over to the digital world.

"Who were they?"

"Doug Manley and his myrmidons, like Big Dan."

"Drug dealers?"

"Small-timers, compared with the Colombians. They're in the past now. Old news."

"So take me through this from the beginning. Amanda actually got involved with Hank Crenshaw."

"They went out a few times. I never talked to her about that."

"Then she dumped him…"

"Yeah."

"Then she got on drugs."

"I wouldn't put it exactly like that. She partied a little bit with Hank Crenshaw, during a weak moment in her life. She wasn't with him long at all, before she got her life on track. She worked hard and became quite the influential activist; but one thing led to another, and this felon kidnapped her…" He wouldn't go that far into Amanda's personal life, with a tabloid beat reporter.

Latham looked at Standt with a greater degree of empathy. He actually had a good heart; it's just that people doubted it due to his hard-boiled and scruffy exterior.

"You know, you look good considering what happened to you."

"Thanks."

"Are you okay now, I mean, with the drugs? The heroin?" He'd heard about the forced shoot-ups with Standt and Amanda. They hadn't been able to keep that one out of the media. After Standt broke the case, the law-enforcement agencies had descended upon the compound and confiscated hundreds of kilos of heroin and other contraband.

Amanda had ended up spending a lot of time at a prominent drug-treatment center in Manhattan. They hadn't been able to keep *that* secret, either. It worked, however.

"I think so. I'm waiting for my test results. I feel okay. I'm not addicted. I'm not a junkie."

"I know you're not. The bastards…ran a torture chamber. They got what they deserved."

That seemed to be the narrative that people focused on, that justice had been served–the universe had righted itself for one brief golden moment.

Latham wanted to swing back to the details. "So you were saying, she dumped Crenshaw, but somehow ended up contacting him again."

"This is just for context, okay? I don't want you printing anything on this. Amanda was injured dancing and developed a problem with Vicodin. That's not uncommon. It's such a powerful opiate that the FDA has tried to ban it. Greedy Big Pharma and their D.C. lobbyists won't allow it.

"At any rate, Crenshaw was able to temporarily relieve the need for Vicodin. That's the only reason she got back in contact with him. He made some promises. Hank got her a couple of prescriptions through a penny-ante dealer named Laney Jentess."

"And *she* was killed? Eventually."

"Big Dan killed her because she knew too much about their drug ring, and Amanda. The taking of Amanda set in motion a set of circumstances that flew out of control. These guys get control *back* by killing. You really should read Katie's upcoming article…"

"My deadline comes before that; as in tonight."

"Then I can't exactly scoop Katie, can I?"

"Hey, who brought you into this story? And Sam Wilcox's big bucks, in the first place?"

"And almost got me killed?"

Even though it was only Latham, with whom Standt did not have to filter remarks, he almost regretted that last one. His wounds were part and parcel of a complicated scenario that finally returned Amanda in one piece to the civilized part of the human race.

"Just tell me this," Latham quipped. Standt chewed on his burger and washed it down with black coffee. The always festive Manhattan eatery crowd bustled around them.

"Crenshaw, for all intents and purposes, kidnapped her off the paddleboard from a boat. He imprisoned her and began shooting her up with heroin. He raped her, repeatedly, while she was drugged."

"The best evidence points to that scenario."

"Does Amanda remember being raped?"

"*I don't know*. Don't print anything in the article on that. I don't want anything personal, you know, the intrusive details about the abuse. People don't need to know that. She's trying to get her life back."

Latham scribbled a couple of notes. "Why? I mean, why the whole sicko imprisonment by an ex-boyfriend? What exactly was the motive? I mean…I know it stems from essential irrationality…but sometimes there's another reason."

Standt paused and put his food down. When beauty, kindness, and caring combine in the same person, as was manifested in Amanda, the modern world often tries to rub it out. The way the Taliban shot that impressive young woman in Pakistan. It's something poison in the air, the way victims are chosen. The human race has terrible flaws. That's just the way it is.

"Power. Control. Evil."

"Turner Espray paid for the helicopter. The one from where Crenshaw was shot?"

"That never happened. Hank was not shot by anyone in that helicopter."

"Then how'd he die?"

"Read Katie's article."

"You know, Standt, I have to make a living too."

"Okay. This is from a source who wishes to remain

anonymous. I heard he fell, trying to run away. The trails in Kauai's mountains are treacherous. They haven't recovered his body. And yes, the helicopter was on Turner's tab. Just don't quote me on that."

"What's Amanda's cell number?"

"You'll never get that."

"I really need an interview. A quote."

"Not happening."

"Thanks. Great. I'll bet Katie got one."

"Katie's willing to talk to you. But only about her role on the last day, when they went looking for me and Amanda in the helicopter. About *her* adventure. Nothing about what happened to Amanda."

Latham was a friend of Standt's, and he had to throw him a bone. He needed Latham for the future.

"What's Katie's number?" Standt gave it to him.

They finished their food and Standt answered more questions; another cup of coffee's worth. Then he stood up, stiffly. Latham walked with him outside.

Standt felt self-conscious with the cane.

"The leg…" Latham said uncertainly.

"It's going to come all the way back."

"Good."

Standt was walking and lifting weights and eating pretty well. His mind was bouncing back; even more important. He was going to spend several weekends with his son Tim. Then they were planning a September holiday together.

Even with the cane, and the profound injuries he had incurred and the abuse he had undergone in Kauai, he probably was still healthier than Latham.

"I'm coming back," Standt said. "Slowly but surely. Did I tell you I'm going kayaking with Tim?"

"No."

"We're taking two weeks in the Lake Tahoe area. Then we're going to Disney World in SoCal on the way home."

Latham was already striking a cigarette pack on the back of his opposite hand to free up a Marlboro. Up went a hand to call a cab. He really didn't like to walk anywhere.

"Sweet. Well you have a great time with your son. Can I call yah?"

"I guess so."

"Actually, one more question." Latham stepped back up on to the curb. "Crenshaw–how did he link up with Manley? It doesn't seem like they would hang with the same crowd. Manley was a surfing thug and Hank a yuppie ne'r do well."

Standt thought for a moment. "Vicodin, I suppose. Crenshaw was desperate to score the Vicodin for Amanda. He went through Manley for that. Then he needed a place to keep Amanda while she was kidnapped, and heroin. He paid Manley for the bungalow." That whole crowd seemed to have gone insane in unison.

"Oh…Just exactly how did you lock on to them?"

"Instincts. And hard work. Luck…" Plus Church's hacker data as they wove through all the possibilities, and Chris K's inside-Kauai information…they'd all played a role, the entire motley team.

Latham stepped into the First Avenue gutter again as a Yellow Cab pulled up. "I guess there's no substitute for that. See yah."

# # #

Amanda was clean. She'd been through the methadone treatment. The cravings for heroin, an all-encompassing impulse that was initially profound, had faded. Cosmetic surgery was taking care of the needle marks.

She just wanted it all wiped away. She would start all over again. They were taking care of it. She hadn't been infected with the viruses–all the tests came back clean. This was the fortunate side of an awful ordeal.

Each morning marked the beginning of a seeking after a kind of purity.

She was sleeping. She was back in Manhattan in one of her father's apartments, near Central Park West. As the sun came up over the trees, she would nurse a cup of coffee, with a little heavy cream and sugar, put on her black Nike sweatsuit, sneakers, and sunglasses, and go running. She never missed a morning.

She went running with Turner Espray twice a week, then they'd have lunch. She found Turner's disguises in Central Park amusing and always changing.

She was getting her vitality back. There were things she didn't remember about Kauai. A therapist told her it was a combination of the narcotic's effects and the skins we grow over the scars of our experience, a kind of natural self-protective armor our minds put up. So we can move on and get through the following days and weeks.

She met Karl Standt in a small outdoor park. It was a beautiful, sunny late-July day that year. Instead of going out to lunch and sitting with the Manhattan crowds, they'd decided to grab some food and coffees to go, and sit somewhere together outside quiet and in the sun.

It was all a part of a process of renewal and healing that they shared.

Standt leaned his cane against the wrought-iron park bench and sat down. Amanda sat on the adjacent bench. She had her long blond hair tied back with a yellow satin scarf, and sunglasses. She wore a purple, fashionable t-shirt from a SoHo gallery, and khaki hiker's pants covered her long crossed legs.

She took off the aviator glasses and smiled.

"You look beautiful," Standt said.

"Thank you. I owe it to you. Everything."

"No you don't. You were the survivor. You survived, you made it. That was the will. You made it through. Now you can forget about it."

Amanda looked away for a moment, at the hardwood trees and the dry leaves through which the warm sun filtered. They heard cars honking, sirens, city noise, but faintly, as though coming from another place way across on the other side of the trees.

"I don't remember much about what happened. I won't read any of the stories."

"It was a bad dream. It's gone. Now you don't have to think about it anymore."

"My father told me that you found me. Everyone thought I was dead. If you hadn't…"

Standt raised a hand. "Just don't think about it. It's all over now."

Standt was thinking about Tim, the twelve-year-old, and how boys are so different from girls. He didn't know whether she thought of it this way, but he felt about her as he would a daughter. He didn't have a daughter. But he was part of the brotherhood now. The men who protected the daughters, against the monsters.

She had fallen into their clutches but now she was safe, back with her family. And he was part of that.

They both sipped on their to-go drinks. Amanda stood up and sat beside him. The sun shined on her face and a breeze came up and she brought up a hand to sweep the hair out of her eyes. Then she kissed him on the cheek. A tear streaked down her right cheekbone.

"Oh no. Not again," she said, and stood up. It was as though she was embarrassed. She was tired of being weak.

That impatience with the aftereffects was a part of the moving on. "I've been crying a lot lately."

"It's understandable."

"How's your leg?"

"It's going to be okay."

She sat back down on the other bench. She smiled. She leaned forward, exuding a special energy. "You look really good. I just can't believe…all that happened to us. But you're a policeman, so…"

"You never get used to the violence. Ever. How's Turner?"

Espray had sent Standt and Katie two red-carpet, orchestra tickets to the Oscar's in Los Angeles. He was already nervous and excited.

"She's good. Really good."

Then Amanda stopped smiling. She looked at Standt.

"Did I kill someone?"

"What?"

Amanda wouldn't want him to lie to her. She wouldn't want to be humored.

"I have…this feeling, a notion, that I picked up a gun and killed somebody back there. Did I?"

"No. You didn't."

"I didn't?"

"No."

The fates killed those men. It was all in the cards Manley and Henshaw had decided to play. And Big Dan. That's how it was going to play out for them.

Amanda seemed to breathe easier. She looked at the trees, and the rectangles of sunlight that rested on the benches where they were sitting.

Standt bent over and removed a letter from a small backpack he had brought with him. The envelope looked official and had the return address of a laboratory on it.

"Well," Standt said. "I guess I'm ready."

Amanda stood up, walked over, and sat beside him. She put a hand on his shoulder. Then he opened up the envelope. It was the result from his HIV and hepatitis test. He was scared to death. Amanda told him to bring it and that she would be there.

He unfolded the paper and read the test results. He looked up. "It's negative. It says the test result was negative."

His chest eased back down and the heartbeat began to slow. Amanda smiled. She laughed, and hugged him. His head fell on to her shoulder where the hair flowed down and touched the t-shirt, where Standt's own streaky tears fell.

He thought a beautiful light shone in Amanda's eyes, the eyes of all the daughters in their grace and glory.

THE END

Made in the USA
Coppell, TX
13 June 2020

27521044R00144